D0982632

The Other
Side of the Tunnel

Candy Bascombe had no idea she was
going to spend such an exciting summer
when she joined the four other children
on holiday in New England. It's not
every summer holiday that you find a
secret tunnel . . . *and* a secret code . . .
and unravel a mystery that began forty
years ago, when other children played in
the woody country round about. Both
boys and girls will enjoy this ingenious
story.

BODLEY HEAD BOOKS · FOR BOYS AND GIRLS

The Other
Side of the Tunnel

CAROL KENDALL

Illustrated by
LILIAN BUCHANAN

LONDON · THE BODLEY HEAD

First Published 1956

Printed in Great Britain by
W. & J. MACKAY & CO. LTD., CHATHAM
for JOHN LANE THE BODLEY HEAD LTD.
28 Little Russell Street, London, W.C.1

Contents

To
CURLEY GREEN

ONE GREY WOOLLEN SOCK

USUALLY CANDY BASCOMBE liked riding in the big new blue Cadillac, but today she felt disagreeable. And when Candy Bascombe felt disagreeable, she didn't let any pleasant thoughts interfere with her mood. She hadn't always been like this. Her mother and father often talked about what a sunny disposition she used to have—before she was ill for so long with chicken pox and whooping cough and measles with complications, one after the other. She was perfectly well now, except that she couldn't seem to recover from her bad temper. At the moment she was determined to make her mother and father suffer for sticking her into this stupid old

'Summer House' while they went off by themselves on a vacation. The place wasn't even really open for the season yet, but Mrs. Summer had said Candy could come a week early, since the Bascombes wanted to set off for Canada on Wednesday. Candy scowled and tossed her fair hair petulantly. The high grey stone wall they were passing made the place look like a prison.

'You'll love it, darling,' her mother said from the front seat. 'All the land behind this wall is part of Summer House. Mrs. Summer said that the children have the run of the grounds—just think, three hundred acres of woods and fields and a real babbling brook, and . . .'

'Huh,' Candy said flatly, 'probably the woods are full of poison ivy and mosquitoes. It'd be just like them.'

'Candy,' said Mr. Bascombe warningly from the driver's seat, 'if you take that attitude at Summer House, the other children won't have anything to do with you.' He swung the car out on the narrow country road to pass an ancient spluttering pick-up truck that leaned crazily to one side. A boy with spiky dark hair and a sunburned face was sitting in the back amidst boxes and sacks of groceries. He grinned and waved companionably at them. The woman driver was plumpish, with pink cheeks and flyaway black hair. Her elbow rested on the door above block lettering that spelled out 'Summer House'.

Candy's lip curled. 'Well, if *that*'s an example of the children, who cares? And you needn't think *I'm* going to ride in a truck, either. What a dump!'

Mr. Bascombe sighed. Then Mrs. Bascombe sighed. And Candy felt quite pleased with herself. They might think they'd got rid of her just dandy, but they'd go away mighty unhappy if she had anything to do with it. She settled more comfortably on the blue upholstery and smoothed her skirt.

Up front Mr. and Mrs. Bascombe exchanged glances and changed the subject. 'Who belongs to that other estate back there—the one adjoining this?' Mr. Bascombe asked.

'I don't know, but that's our turning just ahead,' said Mrs. Bascombe.

In spite of herself, Candy looked up with interest. There were tall iron gates, much like those they had passed in the wall of the other estate, but these were wide open and leaning so heavily on their hinges that it was doubtful whether they could ever be closed again. A drive wound out of sight between borders of thick bushes. As the big Cadillac rolled smoothly through the gates, Candy almost, but not quite, admitted to herself that it might be fun to spend the summer with other kids just playing around these three hundred acres instead of going off with her mother and father to Canada. Anyway, Canada was dull. But it would never do to let her mother and father find out how she felt, or they would always feel free to dump her down somewhere 'for her own good'. Candy made a face out the car window and then gasped. There was a boy standing on the drive, a round-faced boy with glasses on his stubby nose and a squirming black dog tucked under his arm. He was watching them go past, but when he saw Candy's grimace, he first looked astonished and then stuck out his tongue at her.

'One of the inmates?' Mr. Bascombe grinned. 'Looks promising, I must say.'

'Oh dear,' Mrs. Bascombe said doubtfully. 'Mrs. Summer said she always had such nice children every summer. Do you suppose that is her idea of a nice child? Because we could still take Candy with us to Canada if you think . . .'

This was just what Candy had wanted to hear ten minutes ago, but now she wasn't so sure. Somehow she had thought of Summer House as being a dormitory full of girls, and

Candy didn't much like girls. But if there were going to be boys around . . . well . . .

'He wasn't being rude,' she said quickly. 'I was making a face and he thought I meant it for him, so he made a face back.'

'Oh, Candy,' her mother began, but just then they rounded a curve and came upon the house set on a small rise of land. It was a sprawling red brick structure built in the way that children construct houses with blocks, adding a room here and there as long as the blocks hold out. Summer House had had a good many blocks to start with.

Mrs. Summer was on the wide colonnaded portico to greet the Bascombes as the car came to a stop. The girl standing beside her had dark hair that curled in at her shoulders and grey eyes fringed with long lashes. She was dressed in faded tight jeans and a snow-white, over-large sweatshirt. She was very slim and not much taller than Candy.

'How do you do, Candace,' Mrs. Summer said when Mrs. Bascombe introduced them. 'This is Ellen Vance. She has been here for three summers and can put you on to things, such as where the best climbing trees are. Would you like to go off and get acquainted while I talk to your parents?'

'Yes, thank you,' Candy said, and waited for Mrs. Summer to remark on her charming manners or her hazel eyes that were sometimes brown, sometimes green—grown-ups always did one or the other—but Mrs. Summer only smiled and said, 'Run along then.'

As they walked around the house to the play yard in the rear, Ellen said that she was twelve years old and spent her summers at Summer House because her parents ran an hotel, and were terribly busy during these months. Candy looked at her with new respect. To stay in hotels was one thing,

but to *own* one! And Ellen said there was a swimming pool—
and tennis courts. My goodness, if the Bascombes owned
such a place, catch Candy letting them ship *her* out to
Summer House. But Ellen didn't seem to mind.

There would be only four children at Summer House for
the next week, Ellen explained, but after that twelve more
were expected. The other two children were John Addams
and Huggins Pindar. John was Ellen's age and his mother
did the cooking at Summer House—wonderful French
things sometimes, because she was partly French. His father
had died before John was born. Huggins was nine years old,
a year younger than Candy, and wore glasses. He was a real
'brain', Ellen said, and was going to be an animal psychologist when he grew up. Everybody loved Huggy instantly,
from people right down to tadpoles.

'Oh,' said Candy, not at all sure that she wanted to be
classed with tadpoles.

'Are you from Capitol City?' Ellen asked.

'Rosewood. That's the nicest section. *We* think,' she added
hastily as Ellen's eyebrows went up. 'That Huggins—I believe we saw him on the way in. He was carrying his dog.'

'John's dog,' Ellen corrected. 'His name is "Addle". That's
short for Addlepate because he's so silly. When he sees a
car he runs for miles unless you hold him. But Huggy said
he's going to learn dog language so he can train Addle to
behave. That's the secret of being an animal psychologist,
he says. You'll like Huggy.'

'I'll bet,' Candy said, but she said it under her breath.

In the play yard there were four rope swings let down from
the big old maple trees, a croquet set, a badminton net, a
tree house, and a play house equipped with furniture and
dishes for tea parties. Candy, who had some of these things
at home but nobody to share them, began to feel excited.

Then Ellen took her through the big house, which was furnished with enormous tallboys and soft, fat old sofas and chairs.

'You can be my roomie if you like,' Ellen said carelessly as they mounted the stairs. Candy felt pleased inside, but she only said, 'All right' a little stiffly.

Ellen nodded. 'We always double up sooner or later—it's cosier that way. Saves on the housework, too.' She glanced at Candy from the corners of her grey eyes. 'We do our own rooms here, you know. It's supposed to be good training, or something. And we've been helping with the chores because the housekeeper's brother is ill out in Idaho and we said we'd pitch in so she could go take care of him. She'll be back next week.'

'Oh.' Candy gulped. 'Yes. Of course.' She wasn't quite sure how one 'did' a room, but probably it meant making her own bed. She would watch Ellen to see what to do.

Their room was high-ceilinged and pleasant, with soft pink walls and frilly white curtains at the long windows. White tufted counterpanes covered the twin beds, and there were thick blue scatter rugs on the floor. The furniture was enamelled soft blue.

'It's a pretty room, isn't it?' Ellen asked, when Candy said nothing.

'Ye-es,' Candy admitted unwillingly. 'Much better than I expected. It's sort of old-fashioned looking, though.'

'Well, it's an old-fashioned sort of house. Of course, if you'd rather have a different room, you don't *have* to be my roomie, you know.'

'Oh no, that's all right. It's just that we have a very modern house, and—well, I'll get used to this, I s'pose.'

Ellen stared at her for a moment. 'I s'pose you will,' she finally said.

When they started downstairs to say good-bye to Candy's mother and father, Huggins came rushing up to them, his glasses steamed with worry.

'Have you seen Addle?' he gasped. 'He jumped right out of my arms and ran into the woods. I've been chasing him all this time. What will John say? I just took Addle for a little walk, see . . .'

'He'll come back,' Ellen said soothingly. 'Here,' and she handed him her handkerchief, 'clean your glasses and stop panting. You sound worse than Addle.'

'Yes, but what if Addle gets run over or . . . or . . . John didn't *say* I could take him.'

'Well, then,' Candy said coolly, for she didn't see what all the fuss was about, 'why tell him?'

Huggins seemed to see her for the first time. His eyes were very blue when he took off his glasses, and just now they were frosty. 'Who are you?' he demanded.

'This is Candy Bascombe,' Ellen said. 'She's just come. In fact, we're on our way down to say good-bye to her mom and dad. Why don't you come along?'

'I've got to look some more for Addle,' Huggins said gloomily. He drifted off through the rear of the house.

'All that fuss over a dog,' Candy scoffed. 'It's plain silly.'

Ellen looked at her for a moment, but didn't say anything. They went on out to the portico to say good-bye to the Bascombes.

Mrs. Bascombe was full of last-minute advice about which shorts to wear when, and the desirability of wearing jeans while in the woods, and not to forget to take her vitamins every day, and to obey Mrs. Summer in all things.

'I never have the slightest trouble with the children,' Mrs. Summer interrupted firmly. Candy had a feeling that this was so.

At last the Bascombes left, and Candy breathed a sigh of relief. 'Aren't parents a bore?' she asked Ellen.

Again Ellen gave her a look. It was a disturbing look, as though Ellen didn't quite approve of her. Usually Candy didn't care whether other children approved of her or not, but Ellen was different from the children she knew at home. She was more grown up.

'You'll want to get unpacked,' Mrs. Summer said briskly. 'I saw John come back with his mother, Ellen. Would you please run and ask him to help carry up Candy's gear?'

'Sure, Mrs. S.' Ellen dashed off.

'John is the cook's boy, isn't he?' Candy asked Mrs. Summer.

Mrs. Summer gave her the same kind of look Ellen had. 'Ye-es. It's true that Mrs. Addams does all the cooking here.'

'Does he . . . does he *mingle* with the rest of us children?'

Mrs. Summer looked startled. 'Gracious, child, he doesn't have leprosy. Of course he . . . er . . . mingles with the children.'

When Ellen came back with John Addams, Candy recognized him as the boy who had waved to them from the old truck when they passed it. He wore the same grin as before and said 'Hiyah, Candy' when Mrs. Summer introduced them. But Candy knew all about how to treat a cook's boy, even if a cook's boy didn't know how to treat her. Of course, this one looked nicer than Mrs. Staley's little boy, who had used such bad language that the Bascombes finally gave up having a cook altogether. Still, he *was* the cook's boy even if he did have pretty white teeth and a sunburned face, and bright brown eyes under eyebrows that had little wings going up in the centre. He looked scrubbed, as though he had just got out of a shower.

She put him in his place with a gracious 'Very well, thank you, John.'

John stared at her, his funny eyebrows going up in the middle, and then turned to Mrs. Summer. 'Whew, what's *her* trouble?'

Mrs. Summer shook her head. 'John, dear, will you give us a hand at carrying Candy's gear upstairs? If we each take a piece, we can make it in one trip.'

'Sure, Mrs. S.' John grinned at Candy. 'That's a mighty pile of stuff there for one girl. You planning to stay a couple of years?'

'I like to be prepared for anything,' Candy said primly.

'Oh sure, sure.' He scooped up the biggest suitcase and a bag of shoes, and started up the stairs, saying over his shoulder, 'I bet when you go swimming you wear a life belt *and* an innertube. And tie a rope to the shore before you start.'

Candy glared at his back. 'I can swim perfectly well without anything, thank you.'

'Not even water?'

'That's enough, John,' Mrs. Summer said. 'Candy's not used to your teasing.'

Ellen stayed to help Candy unpack, stowing things away in dresser drawers with quick efficiency. Candy was a little disappointed that she didn't inspect all the pretty new things, but then maybe Ellen wasn't used to pretty clothes. Look at what she was wearing—faded tight jeans and an old sweatshirt. And she had only two dresses, skimpy everyday frocks, hanging in the closet. Candy had brought ten. She stood looking at them with pride, then straightened one that was hanging crookedly.

'Do you like clothes?' she asked.

'Oh, sure,' Ellen said off-handedly. She hesitated and glanced at Candy's ten dresses in the closet. 'Old clothes are more comfortable here, though. Doesn't matter when they get torn and dirty. C'mon, let's go find the others.'

Candy trailed a little sulkily down the steps after Ellen. Torn and dirty!

'Tea will be along in five minutes,' a voice said cheerily as they started through the kitchen.

'Goody,' said Ellen. 'Mrs. Addams, this is Candy Bascombe. She's just come.'

'Welcome, Candy.' Mrs. Addams' smile showed small white even teeth. She had black hair and eyes, and her cheeks were pink. 'How nice to have you here! The children asked for a special tea in your honour today instead of the usual snack.'

'How do you do, Mrs. Addams,' Candy said correctly. This was the same plumpish woman who had been driving the old pick-up truck, but she looked somehow different here in the kitchen. She was not much taller than Ellen, even in high heels (imagine a cook wearing high heels!), but she was, well, very sure of herself, like the hostess at a big party, and there was a fragrance of spring flowers about her. Rather too forward, Candy decided as she went outside with Ellen. You might think she owned Summer House.

They rounded a tool shed on the way to the play yard. 'I hate tea, don't you?' Candy said.

'Not when it's a meal.' Ellen smiled. 'Mrs. Summer is English, and in England it's something you eat, like cucumber or banana or sardine sandwiches.'

'Oh! How can you *stand* things like that?'

'You've probably never tasted them,' Ellen said. 'I hadn't before I came here. Let's get the table set in the playhouse.'

Huggins came wandering woefully along and stuck his head inside the playhouse while they were placing the blue and white plates. 'Have you seen him? Addle, I mean?'

'Nope.' Ellen pursed her lips thoughtfully. 'Tell you what we'll do. After tea, we'll all have a grand hunt for Addle. First one to find him wins an extra piece of cake.'

But they didn't have to look for Addlepate. He came tearing into the playhouse just as the sandwich plate started its third round, his black ears flopping, his black curly-haired body wriggling at sight of the children.

'Here, sir,' John ordered. 'Let me see what you've got.' He put out a hand to receive the long limp thing dangling from Addle's jaws. But Addle had no intention of giving up his prize. With a wild roll of his eyes, he took another hold on the thing and started racing around the table, his ears laid back.

Huggins shouted 'Stop!' and Ellen reached out to grasp the black body as Addle dashed past her chair. But Addle, to evade capture, dived under the table.

'Look out!' Candy yelled, but it was too late. Ellen, thrown off balance by Addle's change of direction, fell over backwards. Her feet caught under the table and heaved it into the air. Sandwiches, glasses of milk, cake and cookies went flying in all directions. A sardine landed on Addle's head. It was the only thing that could have stopped him. Addle was extremely partial to sardines. With a shake, he dislodged the sardine, dropped the long grey thing he had been mouthing, and gulped down the bit of fish before any-one could take it away from him. Next in his line of vision was a cucumber sandwich, which went down to join the sardine. He was doubtful over a bit of banana which he found next, but swallowed it on general principles.

Nobody saw what Addle was doing because all four children were examining the prize he had brought in.

'Why, it's a sock,' Candy cried. 'A long wool sock. Mother tried to get me to wear some like that last winter after I was so sick, but I wouldn't. They scratch.'

B

'But where could it have come from?' John asked, puzzled. 'This place is closed up in the winter, so there aren't any children around, and nobody would bring woollen socks here in the summer.' He looked around at the others until his eye fell on Candy. 'Unless you did,' he added with a grin. 'In case it got cold, you know.'

'The sock's tied in a knot,' Huggins said slowly, 'as though somebody did it a-purpose so's he could play with Addle.'

'Well, what of it?' Candy asked impatiently. 'My goodness, all this worry over one old sock. It's not even a pair, though who would want the ugly thick things anyway, *I* don't know.'

Ellen was untying the tight knot. 'It's not an *old* sock. And look how small it is—not as big as mine . . . Wait a minute!' She bent her head over the sock.

'What is it, Ellen?' Huggins demanded impatiently. 'What is that thing?'

'It's a name tag,' Ellen said, her eyes wide. 'Like the ones we have sewed into all our clothes. Only this one has an address too. John, is somebody visiting at Howard Hall?'

John shrugged. 'Search me. Nobody knows anything about *that* place.'

'It's sort of strange.' Ellen bent over the name tape again, and read out slowly: 'Heather Lyne-Howard. And there's an address, too. Tudor Cottage, Chiddingfold, Surrey.'

'There's no such state as Surrey,' Huggins said dogmatically. 'That I know. 'Alabama, Arizona, Arkansas, California . . .'

'Shut up, Huggy,' John interrupted. 'I know where Surrey is. Mrs. Summer's always talking about it because that's where her folks came from. It's a county in England.'

2

ADDLE'S SECRET ROUTE

For a moment there was silence. Then—

'What a silly name, Heather!' Candy said.

'Look who's talking,' jeered Huggins. 'It's no sillier than yours. What does Candy stand for, anyway—Mars Bars?'

Candy stamped her foot. 'You be quiet, Huggins Pindar. And—and, oh, why don't you clean your glasses? They're all finger-marky!'

John was still on his knees beside Ellen examining the long grey ribbed sock. 'Ellen,' he said softly, 'has Mrs. S. said anything about Howard Hall this summer?'

Ellen shook her head. 'Not a word, and I didn't want to

ask. *You* know.' She raised her eyebrows as though there
was some kind of secret about Howard Hall.

'Mmm,' John said. 'She might not like it if Addle goes
over there.' He sat back on his heels. 'Hey! That's very odd.
How *did* Addle get over there?'

His startled tone stopped Candy's bickering with Huggins.
'Walked, no doubt,' she said in a superior tone.

'Over a twelve-foot wall?' John asked. 'He may be addled,
but not *that* addled. And he never goes out on the road, not
since he got his tail run over, so he couldn't have gone
through the main gate of the Hall, even if it was open,
which it never is. So how did he get into the grounds?'
John frowned down at the long sock. 'He had to get this at
Howard Hall. There's no other place.'

Candy brushed at her skirt impatiently. 'Oh, for goodness'
sakes, I never saw so much fuss made about an animal.
What does it matter how the stupid beast got out or over or
under or whatever? All this fuss. You'd think there was some
mystery going on or something . . .' She broke off at the
look on Ellen's face.

'I've got an idea,' Huggins said. He was sitting with legs
crossed, his elbows propped on his knees. He ran his index
fingers around and around the rims of his glasses, an action
that didn't make them any cleaner. 'I have a *good* idea, in fact.'

'Well, go on,' John said. 'We're hanging on every breath.'

Huggins thoughtfully reversed the direction of his fingers
on the rims of his glasses. 'We let Addle smell the sock and
tell him to show us where he got it.'

'I don't know.' John looked doubtfully at Addle, who had
retreated to the door of the playhouse with a cucumber
sandwich which he was licking. 'Maybe he wouldn't know
what we wanted him to do.'

'Well, we could try. Trouble with you is you haven't got

any faith in Addle, see?' Huggins got up. 'Come here, Addle-pate.' Addle glanced up and went back to licking gingerly at a piece of cucumber.

'First,' Ellen announced firmly, 'we carry the tea things in for Mrs. Addams. Everybody grab something, and I'll wipe up the spilled milk that Addle missed. And Candy will want to put on jeans if we go into the woods. Then we'll try Huggy's idea.'

Candy dawdled over her tray. It really wasn't right for Mrs. Summer to expect them all to work, even if the house-keeper *did* have a sick brother in Idaho, and the season hadn't started yet. After all, why were her mother and father paying all that money, if she had to act like a servant girl?

'You'd better hurry,' Ellen said quietly, 'or you'll miss all the fun.'

'All right,' grumbled Candy. 'Though I think it's all very silly getting so excited over a sock and a dog. What's so funny about this Howard Hall place? *Is* there a mystery, Ellen?'

'Well, sort of,' Ellen answered. She finished sweeping the crumbs out the door and put the broom in the corner. 'We're not supposed to bother around over there.'

Huggins stuck his head in the door. 'Hey, you two, better hurry up. We're about to start the experiment.'

Candy almost ran with her tray to the kitchen, but slowed to a dignified walk when she saw that John and his mother were watching her from the kitchen door.

John grinned wickedly at her. 'I was just betting Mom that you wouldn't condescend to carry a tray, and now I've gone and lost my bet.'

Candy gave him a withering glance, but she wished she knew for sure what condescend meant. 'It was a delicious tea, Cook,' she said to Mrs. Addams.

Mrs. Addams' first astonishment gave way to a slow smile. 'Why, thank you, Candy. I like to see children enjoy food. It's the chief reason I come out here every summer.'

John was laughing now, holding his arms across his stomach and doubling over. Candy turned away from him and lifted her head. 'I suppose the pay isn't large. But if you ever want a job, I'm sure my mother would write you a—a—proclamation. That is, after I tell her what good meals you cook.'

John made choking sounds, and Mrs. Addams' smile got broader, but she said, 'Thank you, Candy, but I'm fully employed during the winter and this is just my idea of fun for the summer. If you're going along with the other children, you'd better hurry. I see Huggy making desperate signals around the corner of the playhouse.'

Candy stalked off upstairs to change into her jeans, angry with John, angry with John's mother, and angry with herself. She shouldn't have said that about Mrs. Addams getting a job. It hadn't sounded right at all, and both John and his mother were laughing at her.

It was very quiet upstairs except for old-house squeakings and creakings that made her uneasy. And it was kind of bare and big and shabby, too—not at all like home, where everything was new and pretty and—and . . . Candy swallowed hard to keep back the tears. Ellen should have come up with her to keep her from getting homesick, but all Ellen cared about was that stupid old dog and his stupid old sock.

Only—there *was* some sort of mystery, Ellen had said. Candy stared out of the window as she fastened the beaded Indian belt about the waist of her new jeans. From below came the shouts of the others in the play yard, but Candy paid no attention. She had caught sight of another house in the distance, just showing above the treetops. It looked more like a castle, though, with towers and turrets and things. It must be awfully big to show above the treetops, or maybe it was built on a little hill like Summer House. Why, it must be that Howard Hall place! Candy stared at the bleak towers, grey and stern in the sunlight, and gave a little shiver. Suddenly she wanted to be with the others, even if she didn't like them much. She left the dresser drawer gaping open and ran quickly down the back stairs.

John was in the kitchen drying dishes for his mother. When Candy walked through, he said, 'Well, g'bye, Mom,' slung his tea towel over a rack, and joined her. Candy tried to walk just a little in advance of him, the way her mother swept into elevators with a bellhop in tow, but the annoying John kept catching up with her.

'Hurry *yup*!' yelled Huggins. 'Addle's just *dying* to go. All right, Ellen, here they come. You can let loose of him now.'

As they came around the corner of the playhouse, Addle broke away from Ellen's arms and frisked across the grass towards the trees beyond the clearing.

'Tally ho!' Ellen cried. 'After him, kids.'

Addle, looking around and seeing that they were all behind him, gave a sharp yelp of pure joy and capered on his two hind legs. Then he ran back to John and trotted along beside him, looking up expectantly as though to ask, 'Where are we going, pal?'

John groaned. 'No, no, Addle, *you* show the way! Go on, and we'll follow. Show us where you found the sock.'

'Urf, urf!' Addle yipped and almost fell on his face in joy. John stopped running, and Addle leaped up on him, stubby tail wagging frantically.

'Oh my *gosh*,' Huggins said, 'where's that sock again?'

Ellen gave it to John, who knelt beside Addle. 'Smell the

sock, Addle,' he coaxed. 'Smell it good and then go show
us where you got it. Where did you get the sock, Addle?'
He stood up slowly and then stayed motionless as did all the
others. Addle looked bewildered and went from one to
another, sniffing at them. Candy giggled, but Huggins gave
her a fierce 'Shut up.' After a long moment, Ellen whispered,
'I think he's got the idea.'

'He's going towards the woods,' John answered quietly.
'Let's start after him, now, but not too fast or he'll get confused again.'

The children entered the shade of the oaks and sycamores
with relief, for it was hot in the sun. John spotted Addle's
blackness ahead of them, and they plunged on after him.

'This is the right direction anyway,' Ellen gasped after
a while. 'We're going towards the wall between Howard
Hall and us.'

Candy, at the rear, stumbled over a tree root and cried out,
but the rest didn't stop, didn't even hear her. She pulled
herself up and leaned against a tree, but a rustle in the
branches above startled her and she jumped away from the
trunk. The trees grew thick here; the little afternoon sunlight that filtered through the heavy foliage made everything
look green, as though it was under water. Candy shivered.
This was the first time she had ever been in a wood—you
couldn't count the parks at home, of course, because they
weren't real woods. Besides, there were always people
walking about the paths. But here . . . She had better go
on after the others before they got too far away.

With a sigh, Candy started off. She thought she could hear
voices in the distance as she stumbled along. A lot they cared
about her! Nobody even stopped to look for her. Serve
them right if she got lost and Mrs. Summer had to get out a
search party to look for her. A posse, you called it. And

wouldn't she write a snippy letter to her mother and father about the way she got treated here! Candy paused after a while to listen for the others, but the woods were still except for the restless stir of leaves. Irritably she pushed the damp hair from her forehead. Selfish pigs! At least Ellen might have waited. Well, she'd soon show *them* she wasn't going to run panting after them and their stupid old black mongrel. If they wanted to find *her*, they could search the woods all afternoon. *She* would be back at Summer House eating the chocolates Mother had put in her bag.

With a triumphant smile, Candy turned back the way she had come. It was very still amidst the trees, and the crackle of her own footsteps sounded loud in her ears. She tried walking softly, but the furtive snapping of twigs and underbrush was even more frightening. She started to run.

Low-hanging branches snatched at her, whipped into her face, caught at her hair. When she got back to Summer House, she would never, *never* leave it, except to go home in the big blue Cadillac. She ran until her side began to hurt. Any minute now, she thought. Any minute, I'll be there, and I won't be frightened any more. But there were only trees and more trees, and her side hurt too much to run farther. She leaned against a big sycamore, her breath coming in sobbing gasps. Overhead something scrabbled against the bark. With a leap, she was away from the tree and running again. Oh, if only the others would come now, she would hug them, every one, even that hateful John.

After a few minutes, she slowed down and then stopped. She should have been back at Summer House by now, but the trees grew thickly all around, and there was much more underbrush. The whole place looked as though it had been undisturbed for years. Candy could feel her legs tremble, and her heart thumped loudly in the silence.

'I won't cry,' she said fiercely, 'I just won't cry.' She squeezed her eyelids tightly together for a moment and then opened them. She tried desperately to think of what people were supposed to do when they were lost. At home, in the city, she would have asked a policeman. People in books blazed trails on trees, or unwound balls of string, but she had neither a knife nor a ball of string.

Should she go back the way she had come? The only trouble was, she wasn't sure which way that was. All the trees looked alike, old and grey and menacing. A squirrel came flicking down one of the trunks, saw her and froze.

'It's all right,' Candy quavered. 'I won't hurt you.' But her voice sounded tiny and scared in the green gloom. The squirrel poised motionless.

And then Candy caught sight of something strange through the trees. She blinked twice, but when she looked again, it was still there. Tucked away in a small clearing and covered with tangled vines, was a tiny log cabin! Its door hung idly open on broken, rusty hinges. Candy stood stock-still for a moment. A log cabin here in the middle of the woods? Cautiously, she walked towards it, stirring up a woodmouse who scuttered before her and disappeared across the doorsill into the little house. Candy, who liked mice only when they were in cages, decided to stay outside. The house was smaller than the playhouse where they had had tea earlier, but otherwise the two cabins were much alike.

Forgetting that she was lost, Candy frowned in thought. Why would anybody build a playhouse smack in the middle of the woods? Why, it must have been here for years and years! She walked slowly around the house and stopped in amazement. There was the wall running along close behind the cabin—the wall between Summer House and Howard

Hall! Why, she wasn't lost any more! All she had to do was follow the wall and eventually she would come to the big gates and the drive. That's just what she would do, but first she would have a better look at the log cabin. Wouldn't the other kids be sorry they'd gone off and left her! Serve them right if she never even told them about the little play-house in the woods.

Keeping a wary eye out for mice, she went around and peeked inside the door. A little light came through the vine-covered windows—enough to show a rough table and four stools. A long shelf on the opposite wall had come loose at one end and spilled plates and cups on to the mouldy carpeting that partly covered the rough plank flooring. The planks had rotted away in one corner near the door, or perhaps they had been dug away by some animal. There appeared to be a large hole there, at least a foot across and going down deep. Candy shuddered and drew back, striking the door with her elbow. It made a screeking sound that sent shivers down her back. Gingerly, she pushed it shut. It had a horrid damp mossy feeling, but she forgot that in the next instant, for there was lettering cut into the planks. It was faint underneath the moss, but Candy made out the following:

ND RG UER OU DS AT NTI ON 2

1915

LIB   GUY

LOW   MART

But the first line didn't make any sense! Candy scraped at the moss between ND and RG with her fingernail. Perhaps there were other letters hidden. The moss peeled off all right, but there were no more letters—only the blank wood of the door. She tried the space after RG. More blank wood.

She began to feel excited. Why, it might be a secret language
—a code! It *must* be. And she had discovered it. This *was*
exciting, just about the most exciting thing that had ever
happened. Nobody knew about this old house except herself, and those four names, of course, the ones who had
built it, probably. But 1915 was so long ago that maybe they
were all dead. Well, not dead, but old and grown up and
gone away. How did you solve codes, anyway?

Suddenly she jerked her head away and listened. The
sound came again—a crashing through the underbrush, like
a—an animal, and it was coming towards her. For one
horrified instant she thought: a bear? And then, without
knowing how she got there, she was inside the playhouse,
holding the door closed with hurting fingernails. After long
moments, during which she strained her ears and hardly
breathed, the crashing stopped. Instead, there were sniffling
and snuffling sounds. They came closer. Candy clutched the
bar of the door tighter and tighter. Paws thudded against
the other side of the door and then came the most welcome
sound she had ever heard—shrill happy barking.

'Addle!' Candy shouted. In her excitement at her rescue,
she stepped squarely into the gaping hole in the floor of
the playhouse.

Addle went on yelping joyfully and leaping against the
door, which only banged tighter closed.

'Addle!' Candy called, trying to free her foot which
seemed to have gone all the way to China. 'Addle, go get
the others. Hurry up!' She wiggled her foot and pulled on
her leg, but it was stuck fast. What if there was some kind of
animal down in the hole, a nibbly kind that wouldn't like
her foot in his house? The barking went maddeningly on.

Then she heard voices yelling.

'Candy!'

'Where are you, Candy?'

'Hey, kids, look at Addle!'

'A house!'

The thumping against the door stopped, but the barking went on.

'Hey!' Candy shouted. 'I'm inside.'

Nobody heard her. The babble of voices outside increased.

'Looky, it's just like the playhouse!'

'There's writing on the door!'

'Oh, Addle, stop it! We can't hear us think.'

Candy reached down into the hole as far as she could. That's funny, she thought, it feels like a board down there. She wriggled her foot around, but it seemed to be wedged in between the board and the earth. She yelled again, but the children outside were busily and noisily deciphering the letters on the door, and Addle was still barking and leaping against the door.

Her foot began to hurt from being doubled up. Maybe if she could get her shoe off . . . With sudden energy she plunged her hands into the hole again, found the ties, and gave a jerk. Her foot came out, shoeless, but free. Methodically, she went after the shoe, wiggled it out. Funny about that board. How could a board get buried so deep in the ground? And the big hole leading down to it. It didn't make sense . . . unless . . . She stuck an arm into the hole as far as it would go and felt around. There was the end of the plank, all right, and beneath it, more hole, slanting off to one side.

She jumped up and ran hard against the door with her shoulder. It flew open into the surprised faces of Ellen, Huggins and John.

'Candy!' Ellen cried. 'You were hiding in there all the time. We've been so worried about you!'

'Lousy trick, I'd say,' said Huggins.

'Shut up,' John said, looking at Candy's flushed and streaked face. 'The kid's been scared.'

Candy shoved her chin into the air. 'Have not. But I've just discovered how Addle got over to Howard Hall.' She looked as superior as she could with one shoe off, and added airily into the startled silence, 'He went under the wall.'

'Oh jiminy,' said Huggins. 'She's crazy. How could he go *under* a wall?'

Candy smiled and swung her extra shoe by the ties. 'Through the tunnel,' she said sweetly. 'Of course.'

3

OD YW TAE

'Tunnel!'
'What tunnel?'
'Hey, look what Addle's doing!' Huggins shouted.

They all whirled around to see where Huggins pointed. In the dim light of the log cabin, only Addle's hindquarters were visible in a shower of dirt that he was digging out of the hole. As they watched, he disappeared except for his stubby tail and then that was gone.

'You see,' said Candy, 'he's gone through the tunnel.' But nobody really heard her. All the children had crowded into the playhouse to look down the hole.

'I'm going down, too,' John declared. He dropped flat and began to wriggle downwards head first. After a moment he backed out, his short brown hair sprinkled with crumbs of dirt.

'Too small,' he grunted. 'But there's a board down there —it *could* be the old roof of a tunnel. We'll have to dig out the loose dirt.'

'My gosh,' Huggins said, jigging excitedly from one foot to the other. 'My gosh! I'm gonna take a look.' He sprawled head first down the hole, making puffing sounds. Then he began wiggling his feet. 'Hey, pull me out,' he called in a muffled voice.

Ellen took hold of his feet and began to pull. 'We'll need a shovel if we're going to dig,' she said practically. 'Anyway, it's getting late. Mrs. S. will skin us if we're late for dinner.'

'I'm practically skinned right now,' Huggins panted, emerging from the hole. His glasses were crooked on his nose, which looked stubbier than ever under the dirt streaks.

'Look here!' Ellen exclaimed. She had been stirring around in the pile of broken dishes on the floor. Now she held a thickly-bound book gingerly in her slim fingers. 'Oof, it's awful. Take it, John.'

'Let's see.' John took it eagerly from her, and Ellen wiped her fingers hastily on her jeans. The book was so green and black and white with mould that they couldn't see what its original colour had been. The binding, where it wasn't held together by a rusty metal clasp, had warped out of shape, exposing crinkled brown edges of pages.

'What is it?' demanded Huggy.

John turned it over in his strong hands, while bits of green and black mould flaked off. 'I don't know,' he said slowly. He pushed a little knob on the clasp, but it didn't open.

'Look, there's a keyhole,' Ellen said. 'Maybe we could find the key!'

They all gathered around the clutter where Ellen had found the book and gingerly began picking at the pieces of debris. But though they found the remains of four cups and saucers, a rusty pocket knife, some black-with-tarnish silverware, a tiny handkerchief that fell apart as they handled it, a broken vase, and an old mouse nest, there was no key in the pile.

'Let's go outside,' Candy said finally with a little shiver. The mouse nest had reminded her of the mouse she had seen when she first found the log cabin. It might still be in here.

'What about Addle?' Huggy asked.

As though in answer to his name, Addle appeared at the bottom of the hole and wriggled his way up to them. Safely on the floor again, he shook dirt in all directions and then looked longingly back at the hole, but John led him out of the house by his collar while Ellen and Huggins blocked the door shut with an old log. Addle looked dolefully at them and then sat down to clean himself up.

'Gosh,' Huggy exclaimed, 'we forgot all about this funny writing on the door. Nd rg uer ou, and so on. It's a real code!'

'1915,' Ellen read. 'Goodness, that's—why that's over forty years ago. I wonder who Lib and Low and Guy and Mart were. John, do you know who lived here before the Summers?'

'Nope.' John had dropped to his knees and batted down the tall grass in front of him to put the book on it. 'Get away, Addle. You can't eat this.'

The others gathered around the book, shoving Addle away. John was wiggling the little knob back and forth.

c

Then he tried to pull the clasp out of the lock, but it wouldn't move. His hands were covered with the mould.

'Maybe there'll be secret maps in it!' Candy said. 'Treasure maps!'

'Yoicks,' breathed Huggy.

'I'll bet I know what it is,' Ellen declared. 'It's a diary. Somebody's old diary.'

'Aw shucks,' said Huggy. 'And you're not supposed to read diaries. My Mom says it's not ethical. It's as bad as reading other people's letters, my Mom says. She's strong on ethics.'

'It's all right when they're old and you've discovered them,' Ellen said positively.

'Sure,' Candy chimed in. 'Well, hurry up, John. Can't you break the lock?'

John reached in his pocket for his knife, but Ellen suddenly jumped up. 'Oh my goodness, we can't now. It's too late. We'll have to fly as it is, or Mrs. S. will have a conniption.'

John looked reluctantly from his knife to the clasp, and put the knife away. 'Okay. We'll take it along, then.' Getting up, he looked at the house and the wall and then around the little clearing. 'It's a funny thing, finding all this. I'll bet nobody's been here for years and years. It's sort of creepy, almost. Maybe we're the first ones to see it since, since—well, what's the date on the door? 1915?'

'Yep.' Huggins, still crouched on the ground over the book, ran his fingers thoughtfully around the rims of his glasses. 'I was just thinking—you know what you said about Mrs. S. not ever talking about Howard Hall, and there being something funny about it—well, do you think maybe this has anything to do with it?'

'What do you mean?' Candy demanded. 'What's funny about what?'

'There's not going to be anything funny about anything if we don't go *right now*,' Ellen said. 'Which way is home, John?'

John picked up the locked book with one hand and got out his compass with the other. After a moment, he pointed. 'This way home. I think. We'd better blaze a trail as we go, so we can find the way tomorrow. C'mon, Addle. Home, boy.'

Addle leaped up joyfully and started for the trees.

'Now look at that,' Huggins said with pride as they started after him on the run. 'He doesn't need a compass. Smart dog, Addle.'

'Huh,' Candy sniffed. 'He wasn't so terribly smart at finding the cabin. Goodness, I discovered it a long, long time before you came along.'

John looked up briefly from the oak tree he had paused to mark with his knife. 'We spent a lot of time trying to find you. Then Addle picked up your trail and we got there as soon as possible.'

'Oh.' Then they *had* come back for her, that is, if John wasn't just making it up. She followed silently along behind the others, frowning thoughtfully. 'Thank you,' she said after a while when John had paused to blaze another tree.

'Huh? Thanks for what?'

'Why, for trying to find me.'

John's brown eyes looked amused and his winged brows shot up in the middle. 'What did you think we'd do, leave you around for the squirrels to nibble on?'

Twenty minutes later they rushed into the delicious-smelling kitchen of Summer House. Mrs. Addams, her cheeks pinker than ever from the heat of the stove, shooed them upstairs to bathe.

'If you promise to hurry, I'll ring the gong three minutes

late,' she said. 'You've all got at least three extra minutes worth of dirt on you. What on earth have you been doing, tunnelling?'

For a moment they gaped at her. John recovered first. 'Well, in a *way*. We were trying to crawl down a sort of rabbit hole Addle found. At least,' he went on, carefully truthful, 'I suppose there *could* be rabbits in the hole. We didn't actually *see* any.'

'But it wasn't Addle who found—' Candy began.

'Hurry up,' Ellen interrupted. 'Last one upstairs is a puddle head.'

They scrambled up the back stairs and all arrived at once in a giggling heap at the top. Then John and Huggins raced off down the hall to their room, beginning to unbutton shirts as they ran.

There was a tub as well as a shower in the big pink bathroom next to the girls' room. Candy said quickly that she was going to use the tub.

Ellen only smiled. 'You don't have to clean out a shower. And it's quicker. Gosh, I'm absolutely starved. I could eat three wolves, couldn't you?'

'Uh-huh,' Candy said, 'with mint sauce.'

She was too hungry to soak long, and besides, Ellen was finished with her shower by the time the tub was full. It was lonely in the big bathroom without Ellen. Candy soon scrambled out and dried herself on the enormous bath towel, then thrust her arms into her terry cloth robe and hustled back to the bedroom.

Ellen looked up, her grey eyes wide with surprise. 'Did you clean out the tub?' she asked. Candy pretended not to hear, busy with getting her ruffly pale green dress off a hanger. It was her favourite dress because it made her hazel eyes look green and her hair silvery. 'Because Mrs. S. won't do it, you know. And the cleaning woman only does floors and windows and things.'

Candy shrugged and began putting on her clothes. Just let Mrs. S. try scolding her—just let her! Then she thought about the tunnel and smiled happily.

'Wasn't it amazing how I happened to find that playhouse, Ellen?'

'Amazing,' Ellen said. 'Hurry up. There goes the dinner gong.'

Dinner was laid in an immense cherry-panelled dining-room which Candy had not seen before. Soft candlelight gleamed on the polished table and made sparkling stars on the silver and crystal. John and Huggins, still looking a bit damp about the ears, were already there, waiting with Mrs. Summer.

Ellen asked grace in a high solemn voice, and Mrs. Addams, acting as maid, handed round soup. It had crispy crunchy little squares of toast floating in it. There was a French name for them, but Candy couldn't remember what it was.

'Thank you, Jacqueline,' Mrs. Summer said. 'Are you sure you don't want help from the children? You have enough to do, cooking for these hungry mouths.'

'Not with just this many, Elizabeth,' smiled Mrs. Addams. 'Too many thumbs in the soup plates.' She went back to the kitchen.

'Did you have fun in the woods this afternoon?' Mrs. Summer asked. 'Mrs. Addams said Addle found a rabbit hole and by the looks of you, you'd all been in it.'

'Addle didn't find it!' Candy exclaimed. '*I* did, and it wasn't just a rabbit hole! It was—Ouch!' John had kicked her under the table.

At that moment Huggins upset his water goblet. Ellen

snatched a napkin to mop up and Mrs. Addams arrived immediately with a sponge.

John whispered fiercely to Candy, 'Do you have to rattle off all you know? Don't be a cement head!'

Candy didn't deign to reply. By the time the spilled water was disposed of, and a new lace mat laid for Huggins, Ellen was chattering away about a strange tree she had seen that afternoon. She was sure it was a cottonwood because of all the fluffy white down beneath it.

'We've decided to go in for nature study,' Ellen said with a quick glance round at the others. 'The woods are just crammed with all sorts of interesting specimens. And there are *hundreds* of birds.'

'That sounds a good idea,' Mrs. Summer said. 'Actually, something has come up—some business I must attend to in the city all this week, and I've been wondering how I should arrange matters so that you children would stay amused.'

'Shucks, Mrs. S.,' Huggy beamed, 'you don't have to worry about us. We'll just disappear into the woods all day. Well, except for *meals,* of course.'

Mrs. Summer smiled. 'Fine, then. That relieves my mind. You'll find a lot of books on trees and plants and birds in the drawing-room. The last few years of Low's—Mr. Summer's—life, I wheeled him into the woods every good day and we spent hours and hours bird-watching. You could use our old field-glasses if you like.'

Candy's eyes widened. Low! That was one of the names on the door of the log cabin! Then Mr. Summer—why, of course! This must have been his home when he was a boy. He had built the log cabin then, and the others—Lib and Guy and Mart—were his sister and brothers.

Candy could hardly sit still until dinner was over. The

others must not have noticed when Mrs. Summer said 'Low' because they were all digging into their plates and laughing and talking. Just wait till she told them!

But when dinner was finished and fruit passed around, Ellen said they should help carry dishes to the kitchen. That was bad enough, but then Ellen insisted that they wash the dishes for Mrs. Addams.

'Run along,' Mrs. Addams said. 'Young people shouldn't have chores at this time of night.'

Candy was all set to run along, but the others began dragging out dish towels and aprons despite Mrs. Addams' protests.

'We'll do them in a jiffy,' Huggins said, thumping a plate down on the counter with a resounding thwack! 'I'm a real good dish-washer type, myself. What about you, Candy-Andy?'

'I've never washed dishes, so I wouldn't know,' Candy said disdainfully. 'We have a maid. And an electric dish-washer, of course.' At the mocking look on Huggy's round face, she suddenly felt uncomfortable and wished she could take back her words. Her mother would have said she sounded snobbish.

Mrs. Addams dismissed them firmly before they got to the pots and pans, and they all trooped to the drawing-room at the front of the house. There was a log fire burning in an enormous fireplace, with deep comfortable chairs drawn up before it around a big coffee table. At one end of the long room were bookcases filled with children's books of all kinds, some old, some new.

'Everybody take a book,' Ellen said in a low voice. 'Then we can pretend to be reading if Mrs. S. comes in.'

'Have you got the diary we found, John?' Candy whispered.

His answer was to pull it out from behind the bottom row of books. 'I hid it in here just before dinner. Foxy old me.'

'Yes, but did you hear what Mrs. Summer called her husband at dinner? Low! So he must have helped build the cabin and dig the tunnel!'

'Yup. That's what I figured too.'

'You could have knocked me over with a fingernail,' Huggy said. 'I almost swallowed my tonsils, only I ain't got none. Mebbe those other ones were his brothers and sister, what'll you bet?'

'No,' Candy said instantly, though a moment before she had thought the same thing. 'I don't think so.'

'Then who?' Ellen was taking a copy of *Little Women* off the shelves.

Candy only looked wise and picked up a small pile of magazines. She didn't know who, but Huggy always seemed to make her feel contrary and say things she didn't mean.

Gathered around the low coffee table in front of the fire, they spread out their books and magazines, while John went to work on the diary, if it *was* a diary, with his knife. The hasp was so rusty that it was only the work of a minute to make it fly open. They all leaned forward expectantly as John opened the cover.

The ink was brown on the yellowed paper, but the words were printed large and clear:

Lowell Summer's
PRIVATE JOURNAL
KEEP OUT!

'But that doesn't mean us,' Huggy said hastily. 'Gosh, Mr. Summer's diary! Hurry up and turn the page, John.'

'Umm. I've got to go easy. This paper's awful damp.'

John separated the pages with careful fingers and turned to the next one.

'I can't see,' Ellen wailed. 'Move your elbow, Huggy.'

'What does it say?' Candy asked.

John looked blankly at the page without answering. The others all crowded around his shoulder and then Huggy gave a loud groan.

The brown ink was still clear, and the whole page was printed in block letters. It began:

OD YW TAE MA EP AN DLS FO OU SE RRC RE UN
ER TDG RO ND AI URL WA Y X XA TL ECY SI FE
TF XER OM HE AL TWL ON HE OW THA RD ID
WE SEW IL BE IN LGT OD G I X AC ON EHE WI
LW RK LOA TD GG NG IIF OR IF EE FTN MI UT
SA NET AT ME HI IWL ET EO HE HTR SS AR BU
T'TI LD NG HE ITF IR TS AT STI ON X

4

THE CROSS-EYED DIAGRAM AND
OTHER MYSTERIES

'OH, NO!' Ellen cried. 'We'll never be able to read it!'

'Don't be such a goof,' Huggy said. '*Any* code can be busted. You oughta read about the way Military Intelligence guys go to work.'

'Only we're not Military Intelligence,' Candy pointed out.

'Well, no,' Huggy admitted, 'but then if this Low guy was just a kid when he made up the code, that gives us a better chance.'

John carefully turned another page and then another. They were like the first, printed out in combinations of one, two or three letters. 'Maybe the key to the code's in here somewhere,' he said hopefully. 'We've got to dry this thing out right away. I'm afraid of tearing the pages.'

'It doesn't smell very good,' Candy said, wrinkling her nose.

'Neither would you if you were lying around in the damp for forty years.' Huggy pushed his glasses up on his nose. 'Hey, there's something, John. It looks like a map!'

They stared down at the diagram:

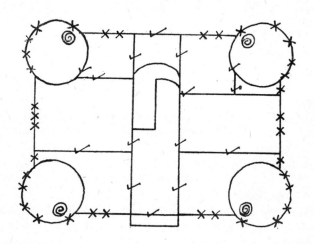

'Looks more like a machine of some kind,' John said. 'What do you think all those x's and check-marks are for?'

'And those round things on the four corners?' Ellen asked. 'With the funny little squiggles in each one? Makes it look cross-eyed.'

'You've got me.' John puzzled over the diagram for a few moments longer and then leafed on. Page after page was filled with the baffling letters.

They came to another diagram very much like the first. There were the four circles, but the lines inside were divided differently, and there were more of them.

'It's no use,' John said. 'We'll just have to break the code to get anywhere.'

'Keep looking,' said Huggy. 'We might come to something else.'

But John shook his head. 'Can't. The rest of these pages are stuck together. Only thing is to get the book really dry.'

Ellen sighed. 'Too bad. Well, anyway, we've found a log cabin and a tunnel—'

'And a sock,' Candy reminded them. 'Goodness, we've forgotten all about the sock. If it hadn't been for the sock, I wouldn't have found the tunnel.'

'Honest to Pete!' Huggins gave his smudged glasses a push. 'You talk more about how you found that tunnel than Columbus ever did about discovering the whole continent.'

'Oh you—you—' Candy couldn't think of anything to call him. She snatched up her magazines and stalked over to the chair farthest from him.

'The way I see it,' said John, 'we all make copies of some of this and then see what we can do with it by switching some of the combinations around. For instance, if you take the first three combinations and turn them around, you get instead of OD YW TAE, DO WY EAT. It doesn't make any sense, but that's the general idea.'

'Yes,' Ellen agreed, 'but it doesn't make sense, either, to have all two-letter and three-letter words. I mean, it would be almost impossible to write anything sensible if you couldn't use any words with more than three letters.'

Huggy was studying the first page. 'I know what the X's are, I'll bet. End of sentence. Who's got some paper and pencils? Let's get started.'

Ellen went to the desk beside the bookshelves to get paper and pencils, while John frowned thoughtfully at the coded page. 'The very first thing we have to do, I suppose, is count all the different letters on several pages.'

'Sure,' said Huggy. 'I remember. Maybe this is one of those codes where they use a "W" for an "A", and all that. You figure out which letter appears most, and that should be "E", because "E" is used oftener than any other letter in the alphabet.' He paused to fan his hand over his short blond hair. 'Only trouble is, I don't remember which letter is used next most often.'

' "A", I think,' Ellen said, passing each of them several pieces of paper. 'Anyway, let's count first and worry about that later. We can each copy down a different page to make it go faster.'

They settled to work and after a while there was only the sound of whispered counting in the room. Candy shrugged and turned the pages of her magazine. They would never work it out. Codes were only easy when you knew what the secret was. All the same, she wished she hadn't stalked off from the others. Now she couldn't go back and help, or Huggy would make smart remarks. At home, her mother would have coaxed her, but it was different here. She leafed another page and then turned back because her eye had caught the words 'Modern Art Institute' as the page flipped over, and her mother and father were patrons of the Modern Art Institute. She read the article with her mind half on it while she listened to Ellen and John and Huggy whisper to themselves.

It was about a millionaire named Peter Slavo who owned a lot of famous paintings and wouldn't let anybody but himself look at them, even when the people of his town got up a petition asking him. Candy remembered hearing her mother and father talk about this Slavo a few months ago. They said he must have something to hide if he was so afraid to have anybody look at his art collection. Candy didn't know about that. After all, if they were his paintings, he didn't have to let the whole town see them if he didn't want to. Though it *was* sort of funny that he didn't let *any*body see them. The article said that nobody else had ever laid eyes on them since old Slavo bought them. It said Slavo was a recluse, which seemed to mean that he stayed in his own house all the time.

Ellen broke the silence. 'I've got way more "E's" than anything else. And next on the list is "A".'

'Me too,' said John. 'What've you got, Huggy?'

'Sssh.' Huggy held his hand up and went on counting, 'four, five, six, seven.' He wrote down a figure. 'I'm not finished, but the "E's" are going to win by a long shot.'

'Well, then.' John rubbed his sunburned nose with the end of his pencil. 'It doesn't look as though Low—Mr. Summer—used substitutes, does it? I mean, if he was using "Y" for "E", then there would be lots more "Y's" than anything else.'

Ellen made a long face. 'Wish he *had* used "Y" for "E". It would be loads easier. I don't know what to do next.'

'Oh, this is where the fun begins,' Huggy said excitedly. 'You just jiggle and juggle and joggle. And then *abacra— acraba—adraca*—Well, anyway, it suddenly comes out.'

'I don't think I'm going to be much good at this.' Ellen put her pencil down and frowned at her paper. 'My brain just feels like a pudding when I look at OD YW TAE MA EP. It sounds like Russian, doesn't it?'

'No spikka da Russian,' Huggy muttered. He plunged both hands into his hair and glared fiercely at the symbols.

'Ellen,' Candy said, 'what's funny about Mrs. Summer not ever talking about Howard Hall?'

'Oh,' Ellen rolled her pencil thoughtfully back and forth on the table. 'Well, she just doesn't ever say anything. I remember the first year I was here, some of us started asking questions about it, and the way she answered, you could tell she didn't want to talk about it. She always changed the subject right away. All we could ever find out was that there's a man named Howard living there all alone, and Mrs. S. knows him but never sees him, and I don't think she wants to see him.'

'But—well, what's so funny about that?'

'It's the way she looks, mostly,' John said. 'When we ask her anything, I mean. Not scared, exactly, but—cautious, I guess you'd say. As if she's—well, braced. It's funny the way you can tell when people don't want to talk about things. Mom's the same way . . .'

'You mean about your Dad?' asked Huggy. 'Yeah, I remember saying something to her about him, and the next thing I knew we were talking about cabbages or some darn thing.'

'*What* about John's Dad?' Candy asked curiously. 'Is there a mystery about him too?'

John shrugged. 'No-o-o, not exactly. But I've never seen any of my relatives. I think there was some sort of family trouble before he died.'

'You're lucky,' said Huggy. 'You oughta see some of the cousins *I* gotta put up with. Boy, are they characters!'

'Well, anyway, I'll bet *I* could find out about Mrs. Summer and Howard Hall,' Candy declared. 'I'm good at finding out things. I always know what I'm getting for Christmas *weeks* before. Mother's given up trying to keep secrets from me.'

'She oughta give up buying presents for you, that's what,' said Huggy. 'Old Needle-nose.'

John looked sternly at Candy. 'Don't you go bothering Mrs. Summer about Howard Hall.'

'Besides,' said Ellen, 'you might give away the tunnel, and then we won't be allowed to work on it.'

'*Might* give it away!' Huggy exploded. 'What about at the dinner table? If I hadn't just accidentally on purpose spilled my water, you'd have spilled the works. Do you have to blabber about everything you know?'

Candy looked uneasily at the three pairs of eyes—brown, blue and grey—staring at her. 'I honestly didn't mean to, but you keep—well, I didn't do it *intentionally*! And you didn't have to kick me, either, John Addams! Not that I'd expect anything else, of course.' The minute she had said it she wished she hadn't. Why did she *always* say the wrong thing?

'And just what does that mean?' Ellen asked quietly.

Candy could feel herself floundering. 'I—I mean that John's rough.'

'Ho-ho!' Huggy said. 'Why you old rough tough, John. Going around kicking the girls. Tell you what, you change places with me at the table tomorrow. I *never* kick.' He looked meaningly at Candy. 'I only pinch.'

John broke in with, 'I've just been thinking about the name in that sock. Heather Lyne-Howard. She must be related to old Mr. Howard, because of her name, but where does the Lyne come in?'

'I think I know,' Ellen said promptly. 'At least, I read somewhere about those hyphenated names. It happens when a girl marries a man and she doesn't have any brothers to carry on her own last name, so she tacks it on to her husband's.'

'Do you mean I could do that if I wanted to?' Candy asked. 'I don't have any brothers.'

'You probably won't have a husband, either,' Huggins pointed out.

Ellen nodded at Candy. 'Sure. You'd be Mrs. Bascombe-Something. Only I don't think people do it much nowadays.'

'I get it,' said John. 'Say Mr. Howard's folks came from England, and there's still a branch of the family over there, only they got hooked up with the Lyne family, and this Heather Lyne-Howard is some sort of cousin to Mr. Howard, even if—'

'Wait a minute,' said Huggy. 'I'm befuddled. Start over.'

'Well, look,' John said patiently. 'Say there are two Howard brothers to start with—back in England, a long time ago, see? One of them comes to America with his wife. That's Mr. Howard's grandfather, or father, maybe. The other brother stays in England and marries somebody named Lyne and tacks her name on to his and you've got Lyne-Howard.'

'That's right,' Ellen said. 'So then the Howards still in England are all called Lyne-Howard, and the Howards in America are just plain Howard, but they're all from the same family.'

'Stop, stop,' Huggy begged. 'I'd rather go on being befuddled.'

'Quick, hide the stuff,' Candy whispered. 'I hear Mrs. S. coming.'

A moment later, when Mrs. Summer walked in, she found Ellen reading *Little Women*, John busy over a letter, Candy deep in a magazine story, while Huggy, his glasses at a rakish angle, was intent on Petersen's *Field Guide to the Birds*.

'It's nine o'clock,' Mrs. Summer said. 'Have you had a pleasant evening?'

'Yup,' Huggy said, holding up his book, and then, noticing that it was upside down, quickly put his hands over it. 'I'm learning all about the yellow-crested bulbsnatcher.'

D

Mrs. Summer laughed. 'Time for bed now if you're going to be any good at bird-watching tomorrow.'

Upstairs, Candy looked out the window before jumping into bed. She thought she could see a faint light just about where Howard Hall stood, but she couldn't be sure. If there *was* a little girl over there, what was she doing now? She must be lonely in that gloomy old house. Heather Lyne-Howard. It was a sort of distinguished name. Almost as nice as Candace Bascombe. Candy yawned and rolled into her bed next to Ellen's.

'Ellen?'

'Huh?'

'What was wrong with Mr. Summer? Mrs. S. said she *wheeled* him into the woods.'

'I don't know. I think he hurt his back once when he was young. Some sort of accident.' Ellen started to yawn, but went on talking through it. 'Better not talk about *that* either. To Mrs. Summer, I mean.'

'What?'

Ellen finished her yawn. 'I said, don't talk about it to Mrs. S.'

'Oh. Is it another mystery?'

'I guess not. But you just *don't* talk about it. Same way you don't ask Mrs. Addams about John's father.'

'*Is* there a mystery about John's father then?'

'Well, if there is, it's none of our business. It's just not *tactful* to keep asking questions.' Ellen started another yawn.

'But you never find out anything if you don't,' Candy protested.

'I know, but you get called nosy if you *do*. Let's go to sleep.'

'All right. G'night.'

'G'night. Snore. Snore,' said Ellen sleepily.

5

CANDY GOES TOO FAR

Bᴜᴛ ᴛʜᴇ next morning when Candy woke up, rain was lashing at the house. She sat up in bed and looked out the window. Howard Hall's turrets were invisible.

'Wouldn't it have to go and rain,' Ellen grumbled sleepily from her bed. 'Just when we've discovered an exciting tunnel.'

'You mean when *I've* discovered it,' Candy said sharply.

Ellen's tousled dark head came farther out from under the blanket. 'Thing I like about you is you're so modest, I don't think.'

This seemed so un-Ellenish that Candy stared at her. 'Well, I *did*. I don't see why everybody has to be so mean about it and claim the credit.'

Ellen pulled herself up the rest of the way and, her pointed little chin propped in her hand, gazed seriously at Candy. 'Look, Candy, Edison invented the light bulb, but do we have to mention it every time we switch one on? Of course you discovered the tunnel. But my goodness, you shouldn't keep on reminding us every fifteen minutes. It gets . . . well . . . boring!'

Candy snatched up her robe and started for the bathroom. 'I'd hate to be as bad-tempered as *you* in the morning, Ellen Vance!' She slammed the door hard.

After breakfast the rain let up a little, but the world was so drippy wet that the children decided to wait until afternoon for their tunnelling, when perhaps the sun would come out. There were various chores to be done like bringing in wood for the log fire, cleaning silver, and washing the breakfast dishes. None of it sounded like much fun to Candy, but she chose to clean the silver because she liked pretty things. By nine o'clock all the chores were out of the way. Mrs. Norland, the cleaning woman, had arrived in a clanking old car, and set to work vigorously with the vacuum cleaner. The children retired glumly to the drawing-room. Candy hadn't forgiven Ellen for criticizing her, and she felt thoroughly cross at everything and everybody, including herself. As cross as when she had had to spend all those months in bed, too ill to do anything. Maybe even a little crosser, because there was nobody to coax her into a better humour.

They got more sheets of paper from the desk and made copies of the first five pages of Low's diary, though Candy grumbled at the task. It all looked perfectly hopeless to her.

'Stupid old rain,' she muttered. 'Stupid old code. Stupid old . . .'

'Gee-*money*,' Huggy complained, 'I can't hear myself think with Candy groaning in my ear. Why don't you just fall in a faint?'

'Shut up, *shut up*!' Candy cried.

Huggy pulled his glasses down on his nose and peered over them at her. 'Brother, what a temper! You oughta put it in a sideshow. Make good money showing off a temper like that.'

Candy scowled at his hatefully cheerful round face, but he only grinned, pushed his glasses into place and bent over the messy sheet of paper in front of him. How *could* anybody be happy when their big adventure was all spoiled because of the rain!

John stopped work for a moment to examine the last part of the diary which was stuck together. He had left it open in his room all night to dry out.

'She's coming,' he announced. 'Look, part of it's unstuck already.'

'Just more silly old code,' Candy grumbled. 'Why would anybody be so stupid as to write a diary in code, anyway?'

'Listen,' John said, rubbing his sunburned nose, which had begun to peel, 'so it's raining and we can't go dig out the tunnel which *you* discovered. Well, *I* didn't make it rain. Neither did Huggy. Or Ellen. Some days it rains and some days it doesn't. So why don't you try being a sport and stop the yammering? Or go read a good book and let us get on with the code?'

'All right, I *will*,' Candy declared. 'You're all just *stupid*, fiddling away with that *stupid* junk!' She jumped up and stalked to the bookshelves.

Huggy cleared his throat. 'I could have sworn I heard somebody use the word stupid around here. Oh well, must have been my imagination. What's that, John?'

'Another diagram, or plan, I guess. Only this one is still a little different from the others. I don't get it. All those x's and check marks, and the wheels on each corner. It just doesn't look like *anything*.'

None of them looked up as Candy walked haughtily out of the room and on upstairs with her book. Her own bed was lumpily made, so she stretched out on Ellen's smooth white counterpane and opened *The Hobbit* at the first page.

But she couldn't keep her mind on Bilbo Baggins in his hobbit-hole. What if the others were working out the code right this minute? Of course, they couldn't really, but if there did happen to be a key to the code in the back of the diary . . . How silly she had been to lose her temper again! It wasn't any fun being up here all alone, and the others probably didn't even miss her. But she did feel cross today.

Restlessly, she got up and went to look out the window. A watery sun was trying to break through the grey mist that shrouded the trees. She could even see Howard Hall now—why, the weather must be breaking! She felt a little tingle of excitement shoot down her back. Maybe they would be able to do some digging this afternoon, after all! As she watched, the mist lifted a little more, and Howard Hall became clearer, bleak and grim with its round turrets. Sort of like the pictures of the Tower of London. Shivery.

Candy blinked. A moment later she tore down the steps and burst into Mrs. Summer's study.

Mrs. Summer looked up from her desk full of papers. 'What is it, Candy?'

'Oh, please—' Candy was breathless. 'Please, could I

borrow the field glasses a minute, Mrs. Summer? I—I want to look at things from my window.'

'Of course. They're in the drawer of the table in the hall. Help yourself at any time, only be sure to put them back, will you please?'

'Oh yes, honest, thanks.' She whirled out of the room, snatched the glasses from the drawer in the hall, and dashed back up to her room.

The big powerful lenses weren't in focus, and she almost dropped the glasses in her excitement as she twirled the adjustment. At last they were just right, but she had to steady her arms against the window sill. Howard Hall sprang into view, so close that she felt she could almost touch it.

'One, two, three, four,' she counted. 'My *goodness*!'

When she burst into the drawing-room again, still carrying the glasses, the others looked up, startled.

Before Huggy could even get his mouth open, Candy said, 'Those whatumyoucallits—the diagrams in the diary— they're Howard Hall!'

'Huh?' The others stared at her.

Candy strode impatiently to the table and began flipping the pages of the journal. 'There! Don't you see? These four round things are the towers. It's Howard Hall, all right. You can come upstairs and look through the field glasses if you don't believe me.'

'By gum,' said Huggy, looking at the diagram. 'Much as it hurts muh, I think she might be right.'

'Of course I'm right.' Candy stamped her foot. 'It's as plain as your nose.'

John thrust one hand through his spiky hair and bent over the diagram. 'Yep, that's what it must be. The check marks could be doors, then. And I suppose the x's are windows. Don't know what these squiggles are in the towers, but the curvy thing in the middle would be stairsteps.' He twiddled thoughtfully with the wing of his eyebrow. 'Now why do you reckon he drew a plan of Howard Hall?'

Ellen shook her head. 'We'll have to work out the code to find out.'

'It's not fair,' said Huggy. 'Us ants plug away doing all the work, and the grasshopper just looks out her boodwar window and makes discoveries. That's not the way it is in all the books.'

'Oh, I'll help you with your old code,' Candy offered magnanimously. 'It's probably quite simple, really.'

Huggy stared broodingly at her. 'Yuh know, if you take my advice, you'll never enter a popularity contest.'

Candy tossed her head. 'Huh! Who wants to be popular?'

'Don't start squabbling again,' Ellen said. 'Let's get to work.'

But by lunchtime they were no further ahead with the code and only had a litter of attempted and discarded solutions strewn about them. The sun had burned away the mist and dried the ground enough so that they could eat under the trees in the side garden. Everybody helped Mrs. Addams carry out food and dishes to the rustic table overlaid with a red-checked tablecloth, and when lunch was finished, they all rushed the dishes back to the kitchen. Ellen scraped and stacked the plates while John put away leftovers. Huggy drew the dishwater and sprinkled too much detergent in it. The hot water steamed his glasses, so he pulled them down on his nose and peered over them.

'Dish towel in the drawer right there.' Huggy motioned to Candy, who had been standing helplessly in the middle of the room.

Mrs. Addams, pushed out of the way, shook her head admiringly. 'If this goes on much longer, we'll all have nervous exhaustion. I've never seen such a display of energy. What's up?'

Candy didn't need Huggy's warning glance this time. 'Well, if we're going to work, might as well get it done fast, that's what *I* say,' he declared.

When the dishes were finished, Huggins went out first while the other three kept Mrs. Addams in conversation so that she wouldn't see him making for the tool house near the kitchen. Mrs. Summer had left for Capitol City several hours earlier. When John, who was keeping an eye on the tool shed, signalled that the coast was clear, they all said good-bye and went out to the play yard where Huggy was waiting with two buckets, a spade and a trowel. Addle capered round and round with excitement.

'He knows something's going on, all right,' said Huggy. 'Good ole Addle, you're a smart dog, all right, all right. You can take us right back to the tunnel, can't you?'

'Not . . .' Candy began and then thought better of it.

It took them almost an hour to find the little log cabin, however, because some fallen branches confused them and they got off John's blazed trail. The woods smelled clean and sweet after the rain, and Candy wondered how she could have been frightened of the friendly trees.

At last they came to the tiny clearing by the vine-covered wall, and there was their log cabin, undisturbed from yesterday.

'John can dig first,' Ellen announced, 'and the rest of us can haul out the dirt in the buckets and clean up the cabin a little. Look what I sneaked out of the house.' From her belt, hidden by the voluminous sweat shirt, she produced a whisk broom and a hammer, and from her pocket, a handful of nails. 'We should have some water and soap, but I couldn't manage without looking too fat. Anyway, Huggy, you can nail the shelf up again, and I'll carry all this broken stuff out, and Candy can start whisking.'

'Bossy old Ellen,' Candy muttered, but nobody paid any attention.

John set to work, but he was soon steaming in the close air of the cabin, and Huggy took over while Candy went sulkily outside at Ellen's direction and pulled some of the vines away from the two windows to let in more air.

'Gee-whammy,' Huggy panted, his face red with exertion and his glasses awry, 'this isn't so very blamed easy, I'd say. But we're getting somewhere. Don't ask me where the somewhere is, though. Hey, Addle, get out of here, or you'll get your nose spaded off your face.'

Addle crouched by the ever-widening hole and barked. Then he began scratching furiously at the dirt, sending a shower up in Huggy's round face.

'Call him off,' yelped Huggy. 'Hey, John, call off your dorg.'

But Addle went deliriously scratching downwards in a storm of flying dirt and wriggled out of sight at the bottom of the hole.

'My turn,' said Ellen, taking the spade from Huggy.

'What about me?' Candy asked indignantly. A moment before, she had hoped to get out of blistering her hands, but if they were all going to ignore her . . .

Huggy glanced up in astonishment. 'You mean you ack-shully *want* to do something? Ellen, give her the spade quick before she changes her mind.'

Candy glared, and seized the spade. She would soon show them she could work twice as hard as they could. She lifted a spadeful of dirt and let it slide into the bucket. The hole was almost two feet across now, and three feet deep. Down at the bottom you could see where the tunnel sloped off sideways beneath the board. Lots more had to be dug out before anything larger than Addle could get through. Candy got up another spadeful and then another. Her back ached already, but she gritted her teeth. She wouldn't stop until somebody took the spade away from her.

It took ages to fill up just one little bucket. Sweat was streaming down her face, blearing her eyes, and her curly hair was plastered to her head. The others were outside the cabin laughing and talking. A lot *they* cared that she was working herself to death. Huggy came in and took the first bucket away to empty it, but he didn't say anything. Grimly, Candy started to fill the second bucket. If her mother could see her now, she'd faint smack away and then jerk her out of Summer House so fast her teeth would rattle. Candy smiled to herself and dug harder. Maybe it would be fun to get her hands all blistery and ugly and turn into a regular tomboy, just to see—

'*Hel*-lo.' The hollowed lilting voice startled Candy so much that she dropped the spade and spun around. But nobody was there. The others were still outside—she could hear them clearing away dead branches.

'Hel-*lo*?' The inquiring voice was right in her ear! Frightened, she stared around the log cabin. Nobody! Nothing!

'Wh—what—who is that?' Candy quavered.

A tinkly little echoing laugh sounded in her ear. It was coming from the hole!

'I'm on the other side of the wall. You live in that big house over there, don't you? I say, is there really a tunnel? What fun!' The voice was quick and clipped and—why, it was like English children in the movies!

'Are you Hea—Heather?' Candy stammered.

'Yes. However did you know? Oh, of course, my sock. Is this your dog? I followed him yesterday and that's how I found this place.'

'It's John's. He's—Listen, can you get through that end?'

'I don't think so. Too many logs piled around and there's just the *teeniest* hole way down underneath. Wait a moment.' There was a sound of wood thumping against wood and then a short silence.

'Hel*lo*?'

'Yes?' said Candy. This was like a dream, but the disembodied voice went on quite cheerfully.

'Too many logs, you see, and I'm not supposed to be out. I came through a window. Uncle Guy will be in the most terrible rage if he finds me gone.'

'Wait a minute,' Candy called shakily. 'I'll get John and the others.'

'Do hurry, then. Uncle Guy has a frightful temper.'

Uncle Guy! Another of the names on the door of the log cabin! Candy scrambled to her feet and lurched to the door. 'John! John! Come here, quick.'

John took one look at her face and came running, followed by the others.

'What's the matter, kid?'

'It's Heather,' Candy babbled. 'She's at the other end of the tunnel but she can't wait because her Uncle *Guy* will be mad—she sneaked out of the house—and there are logs blocking her end of the tunnel. You talk to her.'

'My garsh,' Huggy breathed, but John flung himself down by the hole.

'Hi there,' he shouted.

'Hel*lo*? Are you John? Look here, I can't stay any longer, really I can't.'

'Listen, can you come back tomorrow?'

'Yes, but I can't say when. Uncle Guy—'

'Okay, but listen. Whenever you can, try to move some of those logs, will you do that? Then we'll tunnel through to you.'

'All right, but there's a jolly lot to move. I can't promise *when*. Uncle Guy would be furious if he found out.'

'He won't find out if you're careful. Hey, are you—that is, are you *all right*?'

'Certainly. Except—are there *really* rattlesnakes in these woods?'

'Lordy, no. Just some little garters and they're real friendly. I've got two in my room. Who told you that?'

'Uncle Guy. But I *must* go now. Whistle for your dog. Good-bye!'

'Wait!' John called, but there was silence except for a few short barks. John whistled and whistled again. There was a scrabbling sort of sound, and in a few minutes Addle emerged from under the board and scrambled up the steep side of the hole.

John sat back on his heels and rubbed his forehead bewilderedly. 'Whew!' He looked around from Ellen to Huggins to Candy and then grinned, his teeth very white in the dim light. 'You're the doggonedest girl for finding excitement I ever saw. How do you do it?'

'I th-thought it was a ghost,' Candy confessed. 'Scared me to death.'

'But she said Uncle *Guy*!' Ellen cried. 'And that's one of the names on the door of the cabin. So—My goodness, Candy, tell us exactly what she said and what you said. Let's go outside and sit down. I'm simply *weak*!'

They blocked the door shut to keep Addle away from the tunnel, and Candy recounted her conversation with Heather.

She was a good mimic and gave all of Heather's words in the clipped accents the English girl had used. When she finished, the others remained staring at her.

'Sounds t'me,' said Huggins, taking a turn around the rim of his specs with his grubby forefingers, ''s though Unkie Guy is an A-number one, double-dyed, large-sized louse.'

'Rattlesnakes!' Ellen snorted. 'I'll bet there isn't a rattlesnake in a thousand miles from here.'

'That's right,' John frowned. 'He's trying to scare her into staying out of the woods, and that doesn't make sense.'

'Maybe he's afraid she'll get lost,' Huggy offered dubiously.

'Don't be silly,' Candy scoffed. 'He's—he's *sinister*. I just feel it in my bones.'

'That's silly too,' said Huggy. 'How can you tell about somebody you've never even seen?'

'Well, *I* talked to Heather and you didn't.' Candy tossed her head. 'I could tell by the way she said those things about Uncle Guy that he's mean and wicked. Besides,' she added triumphantly, 'there must be a good reason Mrs. Summer won't have anything to do with him!'

'You know,' John said suddenly, 'if there're lots of logs blocking the other end of the tunnel, I'll bet there was another cabin just like this one over the wall!'

'Of course,' Candy said loftily. 'Are you just figuring that out?'

John drew a deep breath and turned his head slowly towards her. 'Sometimes, Candy, sometimes I feel like wringing your little neck.'

'I just dare you to try!'

'You need any help, John, just call on me,' said Huggy. He stuck out his jaw ferociously.

Ellen jumped up. 'Well, *I'm* going to dig. Maybe we'll get all the way through by teatime!'

But work as fast as they could, they had still not got the hole deep enough for anybody to crawl into the tunnel itself when it was time to go back to Summer House. Candy complained that Addle slowed them up and should be left at home, but Huggy said that if Addle stayed home, so would he. John only frowned and went on making a list of the things they should bring with them the next day: pick-axe, flashlight, a thermos of water . . .

'Anything else?' he asked. 'Okay, let's go. It's late.'

They made a dash home through the woods with Addle frisking between their legs and almost bringing them down.

After an enormous tea, which they coaxed out of Mrs. Addams and ate ravenously in the playhouse, they were too tired to move. Candy's soft palms were blistered and hurt so much that she felt like crying. Addle snuffled around looking for crumbs without much success, eyed the table sadly, and finally settled on the floor, head on his front paws, and sighed an enormous, heart-breaking sigh.

'He's faking,' John said. 'I personally fed him two peanut butter sandwiches.'

'And I gave him a cookie,' said Ellen.

Huggy grinned. 'He had three carrot sticks from me and a piece of celery. What a phony!'

Candy felt her face going pink. When Addle had begged from her, she had pushed him away with her foot.

'I don't think animals should be fed at the table,' she said. It was the wrong thing again, but she couldn't help going on in the face of their shocked gaze. 'In fact, animals shouldn't be allowed around when people are eating, specially when they smell like Addle. He's *dirty*!'

'Oh boy,' Huggins breathed, 'here's where the wringing starts.'

John stared thoughtfully at Candy. 'You know,' he said in a deadly quiet voice, 'if it weren't for my Mom's expecting me to be a gentleman, I'd sure take a poke at you.'

'Doesn't surprise me,' Candy said defiantly. 'Must be pretty hard for the son of a cook to be a gentleman.'

John stood up. 'Listen, *you.*'

'All right,' Ellen cut in sharply. 'Candy, apologize to John right this instant.'

Candy felt her insides curl up. She hadn't meant to say it—she wished she hadn't, but she just could not apologize . . .

'Go on,' Ellen said coldly.

'All right.' Candy tossed her head. 'I'm sorry your—your *Mom* is a cook. So there.'

Ellen stood up. 'I guess that's just about the end. Come on, kids, let's take the dishes in to Mrs. Addams. My Mom's a cook too. She cooks breakfast, lunch and dinner every day. What about yours, Huggy?'

Huggins began stacking plates. 'My Mom's a terrific cook, let me tell you. Talk of the town, she is. Pindar's Mom sure can wiggle a frying pan, they all say.'

They went out, leaving Candy with scarlet cheeks. Addle started to follow the others, looked back at Candy and whined softly. She didn't look at him. He trotted over to her and stood staring up at her, one eyebrow cocked sympathetically, his stub of a tail wagging. When she didn't move, he nuzzled at her hand, tentatively licked her little finger.

Candy suddenly knelt beside him and laid her hot face against his silky hair. 'Oh Addle,' she cried, 'why do they all have to be so hateful! They know I didn't really mean it!'

Addle stood patiently a moment and then turned his head and licked soothingly at her ear.

'I'm s-sorry I didn't give you anything to eat,' Candy sobbed.

Addle made embarrassed grumbling noises in his throat and tried to lick her hair. Candy wrapped her arms around him and cried for a long time into his fur.

Finally she mopped her face and walked slowly towards the kitchen door. There was no sign of the others. Mrs. Addams glanced at her tear-streaked face and said cheerily, 'You'd be surprised what wonders a good hot bath will do to tired bones. Run along and soak and then come back and talk if you like. The others have gone walking down the road to meet Mrs. Summer.'

Candy nodded and slowly climbed the back stairs to the bathroom. Her towel lay huddled on the floor where she had dropped it the night before. There was a ring around the tub and nasty grit caked on the bottom. How could she take a bath in *that*? She sat on the edge of the tub and looked glumly out of the window. There were the cold turrets of Howard Hall rising out of the trees just as before. Somewhere inside that forbidding castle of a house was Heather with her Uncle Guy, perhaps even locked in her room. She might be looking out of one of those tiny windows towards Summer House right now, wondering about the girl she had talked to through the tunnel. There was a tiny crumb of comfort in the thought.

With a sigh, Candy got up and began looking around for something to clean the tub with. There was an old washcloth hanging over the waste pipe, and some cleanser in the cabinet. Candy got to work, though the cleanser stung her sore palms.

Then she filled the tub with hot water, poured in a packet

E

of her birthday bath salts, and peeled off her clothes. She soaked until the water was cool, but this time she stayed in until the water ran out and then washed the tub with fresh water. Her own bath towel felt clammy wet, but she didn't quite dare to use Ellen's, which was hanging bone dry on the rack. Instead she did the best she could with her hand towel and went forlornly off to her room to get into her pyjamas. It would be comforting to go down and talk to Mrs. Addams, but—well, she couldn't very well after what she had said to John.

There was a big sheet of paper pinned to Ellen's bedspread just above some little chunks of mud.

WHEN PEOPLE LIE ON OTHER PEOPLES
BEDS THEY SHOULD FIRST TAKE OFF
THEIR SHOES AND SECUND STRAIGHTEN
THE BEDSPREAD. THANK YOU.

                    ELLEN VANCE.

Candy read the message with a sniff. Ellen couldn't even spell 'second'! She gave the bedspread an indignant swipe with her hand. There! You could hardly see the dirt unless you had a magnifying glass. Imagine making such a fuss over nothing!

A little later there was the sound of a car and lots of laughter outside. Candy put *The Hobbit* on the bedside table, turned over, and pulled the sheet up to her ears. She heard Ellen come into the room and go out again to take a shower, but she made no movement. Then Ellen came back to dress. There were swishing sounds and some thumps, followed by a long silence.

'Candy?' Ellen said finally. 'It's almost time for dinner.'

Candy lay perfectly still, her eyes fast shut. A long pause and then a soft warm hand felt her forehead. Candy gave no sign. The hand was withdrawn.

'I know you're not asleep,' Ellen said. 'You're not breathing that way. If you don't want any dinner, I'll tell Mrs. S. you're too tired. Okay?'

Candy didn't move and tried to breathe differently.

'John said he didn't want any old apology, so that's that. But my goodness, don't you *want* to have friends? You keep on making everybody sore.'

'You're all against me,' Candy said into her pillow.

'Don't be silly.' Ellen's voice was sharp. 'Listen, we're all stuck with each other for the summer, so we might as well make the best of it.'

'You like the others better than you do me,' Candy mumbled.

Ellen was silent for a moment. 'Well, they make it a little easier. Trouble is, you say anything you like to us, but you get mad when we tell you what *we* think.'

Below them, the gong boomed for dinner.

'Do you want me to bring you something to eat?' Ellen asked gently.

Candy shook her head against the pillow.

'All right, then. We're going to work on the code again tonight, if you're interested.'

Candy shook her head again. Ellen's footsteps went towards the door, then paused.

'John got the bright idea of looking up Guy Howard in the telephone book,' Ellen said. 'Just to check up, sort of. Funny thing is, the only Guy Howard in the book lives in Capitol City. But we found something else—are you interested?'

Candy hesitated before nodding her head.

'Well, we looked all through the rest of the Howards until we found the one living at Howard Hall. Guess what his first name is!'

Candy opened her eyes. 'Is it one of the names on the log cabin door?'

'Right the first time. It's Martin!'

6

A NEW DISCOVERY

CANDY AWAKENED with the first streak of sunlight across
her bed, and sat upright. There was something she
must do, but she couldn't remember what it was. The morning mist was clearing away fast, leaving the turrets of
Howard Hall glinting in the sunlight. The tunnel and
Heather! It was going to be an exciting day. Then she
looked across at Ellen's dark hair fanned out on her pillow,
and remembered what she had forgotten. It wasn't going to
be an exciting day at all, because she had decided last night
before she went to sleep that the others could have their old
tunnel and she would make Mrs. Summer telephone her

mother and father to come and get her. They weren't
starting out for Canada until tomorrow and when they heard
how miserable she was, they would never go off and leave
her.

She looked wistfully out of the window again, at the mys-
terious towers across the treetops. If she went home, she
would never see Heather, never find out why Uncle Guy
told her there were rattlesnakes in the woods, never know
if the code got worked out or what secrets it held, never . . .

She reached out her hand for the box of tissues on her
bedside table, and almost knocked something over. It was
a small thermos bottle, and beside it was a plate of cookies
topped with a paper napkin on which was printed:

IN CASE YOU GET HUNGRY IN THE NIGHT.
WAKE ME UP IF YOU GET LONELY.
                                    ELLEN.

The thermos contained hot chocolate, still warm. Candy
poured some into the plastic lid and took a swallow. Then
she picked up a cookie and leaned back against her pillow.
Ellen must be feeling sorry she'd been so mean. Maybe—
well, maybe she wouldn't have Mrs. Summer call up her
mother after all. At least she might wait until after lunch . . .

Ellen yawned and stretched and slowly opened her eyes.
'G'-morning,' she said sleepily.

'Good morning,' Candy returned gravely. 'Thank you
for the stuff to eat.'

''S all right.' Ellen yawned again. 'You may be a goose,
but I suppose even geese get hungry.'

'Oh.' Candy looked at the cookie and then carefully laid
it back on the plate. 'If that's the way you feel about it. I
thought maybe you wanted to be friends again.'

'Oh for goodness' sake, stop being such a dope. Toss me a cook, if you're too proud to eat them. Thanks, pal.' She took a bite. 'Mmm. Mrs. Ad's finest. She's terrific.'

'They are very good,' Candy said, examining a fold in her sheet.

'Yep. Better eat up before I snag all of them. We've got to keep our strength up for digging.'

'You mean,' said Candy, running her finger down a valley in her sheet, 'you mean that I'm invited along?'

Ellen stared at her. 'Well, there aren't any special engraved invitations saying "Digging from two to four". For heaven's sake, Candy, we're just all going to go and *dig*. Toss me another cook, old girl. My stomach's full of empty crevices.'

After breakfast, at which Huggy and John gruffly said 'Hello' to Candy and then more or less ignored her, they all collected in the play yard where Huggy had dumped the spade and buckets, a broom, a trowel, a short-handled pick, a sickle and a flashlight. John parcelled out the tools amongst them. Candy self-consciously patted Addle, who was doing his usual frolic and dance around them.

This time they followed the trail without any trouble and soon reached the log cabin. They drew straws for order of digging. Ellen was first. John pulled a hammer out of his hip pocket and announced that he was going to patch the roof where some of the shingles were flapping loose. Huggy decided to whack at the long grass with the sickle.

Candy stood back uncertainly while the rest got to work. 'What should I do?' she asked when John had crawled up on the roof and started pulling vines away.

He glanced down at her. 'Could you cut some bark off that fallen tree over there?' He pointed to the edge of the clearing. 'I need some shingles for the roof.'

'All right,' Candy said doubtfully. 'I'll need a knife or something, won't I?'

'Yep.' He tossed his scout knife down to her. 'Thanks.'

By eleven o'clock, when they had each had three turns at digging, there was enough room for Huggy, who was the smallest, to wriggle in and flash his torch into the tunnel.

'Well, hurry up,' John said. 'What do you see?'

'Lots more work,' came Huggy's muffled reply. 'There's a bunch of dirt piled up 'bout six feet along—must've been a cave-in some time or other. The tunnel's narrower right there.' There was silence for a moment and then he added, 'There's a coupla planks missing from the roof. Prob'ly buried under the dirt.'

'Heave yourself out then, and let's get on with it,' John said. He grabbed one of Huggy's legs, Ellen the other, and they tugged him out.

Huggins sat up and brushed the dirt crumbs out of his short fair hair. His glasses were steamed and grimy. 'Swell tunnel, when we get it fixed up. Just big enough to walk through if you bend over. All boarded along the sides and top. And you can see how Addle got through over the top of the dirt pile.'

They worked for half an hour longer deepening the hole down to the tunnel entrance and then it was time to go home for lunch.

'I wonder where Heather is,' Ellen said thoughtfully. 'Do you suppose Uncle Guy wouldn't let her out of the house?'

'Never mind,' said John. 'If she doesn't show up this afternoon, we'll go through the tunnel and find her.'

Candy shuddered. Digging a secret tunnel was one thing, but setting off through the dark trees on the other side of the wall to find Heather, perhaps being caught by Uncle Guy . . .

At lunch Mrs. Summer, back from Capitol City, reported that Candy's mother had just rung up to ask if Candy was enjoying herself.

'Boy oh boy,' said Huggy, 'you'd never catch my mother phoning up about little old *me*. She just breathes a great big ole sigh of relief and says, "Poor Mrs. Summer, what *she's* going through".'

'And well she might,' Ellen said. 'If I were your mother, I'd look out for a Mrs. Winter to take you off my hands for the rest of the year.'

Huggy groaned. 'Thing I like about this crowd is they never leave you in any doubt about their love for a guy.'

'Surely,' said Mrs. Summer, 'surely somebody can think of a nice remark for Huggins.'

'I can,' Candy spoke up. 'His glasses are clean for a change.'

Huggy bowed low and almost put his nose in his strawberries and cream. 'Thank you, Modom.'

'By the way,' said Mrs. Summer, 'Mr. Jacobs was looking for the sickle this morning. Have you children seen it?'

'Oh, we borrowed it,' Ellen said candidly. 'We found a nice sunny spot in the woods, but the grass was too long and prickly.'

'Thought we might build something there,' added John carelessly, 'if we can have some of that old lumber in the tool house.'

Lunch over, John begged sandwiches and thermoses of lemonade from his mother for tea in the woods, and they hurried back to the log cabin, Candy trailing in the rear.

At three o'clock the hole was big enough for John to crawl into the tunnel and attack the pile of dirt that blocked the middle. Ellen had thoughtfully brought along some stubs of candles, and one of these stuck in the dirt gave

enough light to work by. It was steamy hot in the close air.
When John dragged himself out with the two buckets full,
he threw himself on the grass outside the log cabin and
panted.

'As bad as Addle,' Candy said jokingly, but John only
turned his face away.

They weren't being at all nice to her, Candy thought,
even though she was as nice as pie to them. Just because
she had said some things she was sorry for the minute after.
Why couldn't they understand that she had only been feeling
terribly cross and unhappy yesterday? Everybody felt out
of sorts sometimes. She leaned over and patted Addle, who
was lying glumly with his head on his paws. He wasn't
allowed to go through the tunnel for fear Uncle Guy might
see him on the other side and follow him back to the wall.

Ellen filled her two buckets and then it was Candy's turn
to crawl into the tunnel. The candle was stuck into the
caved-in earth, its flickering light casting weird shadows in
the gloom. She scooped away until she had filled one bucket,
and then sat back on her heels to rest her aching arm. It
was hot and damp in here, though it seemed cool when you
first came in. Candy looked thoughtfully at the pile of dirt.
It would take ages to dig all that out into buckets. There
ought to be an easier way. She frowned.

Why not spread the earth all along the tunnel floor?
Scattered out that way, it wouldn't make the floor much
higher. She set to work again with the trowel. Not that the
others would *appreciate* what she'd thought up. Huggy
would probably say she was lazy, and Ellen might think she
should have asked them first. John would just look mulish.
She paused with the scoop raised and considered. No, that
wasn't quite fair. John was—well, he was sort of *nice*. And
dependable. And his mother wasn't very cookish, either.

She wasn't at all like that awful Mrs. Staley who used to cook for the Bascombes and sometimes drank the cooking wine. And there was the mystery about John's father, too. Maybe he had had enemies, and Mrs. Addams became a cook as a . . . well, disguise, to keep the enemies from finding her and John.

She plunged the trowel into the dirt again and scattered it around the floor behind her. Her arm ached and her hands stung, and sweat was trickling into her eyes. She had certainly done two buckets' worth by this time. But if she appeared with only one bucket, the others would think she was trying to get out of work, even if she showed them her new idea. Grimly, she set to work to fill the second bucket. The dirt was harder to dig out now, the farther she went into the pile. After ten minutes she thought her fingers would drop off. She used her left hand for a while. Sweat ran down her face and dripped on to her arms, but she wouldn't quit until that second bucket was full.

'Hey,' came John's voice from the tunnel entrance. 'You all right? Come on up for air.'

'Right,' Candy gasped. She dug once more, but her arm was so tired the trowel wobbled and fell out of her hand.

There were scrambling sounds and then John appeared behind her. 'You've done enough,' he said. 'Here, I'll take the buckets.'

'I—' Candy was too tired to talk. She pointed to the earth she had scattered on the floor.

John pursed his lips and then nodded approvingly. 'Good idea.'

She smiled, suddenly happy. Then he added gruffly, 'Now don't go beating your chest about it, or you'll spoil it. See?'

Candy gave a disdainful sniff, the warm ball of happiness inside turning hard and cold. Why, she'd been almost ready to tell him she was sorry for what she'd said yesterday, but if that's the way he was going to act, he didn't deserve an apology. She picked up the trowel and jammed it into the remaining pile of dirt. It made a funny little tinging noise.

'That sounded like metal!' John said. 'Here, let me have a dig.' He seized the trowel. Dirt rained through the air in all directions for a few moments. Then he sat back on his heels. 'Okay, you want to pull it out, whatever it is? It's your find.'

Candy shook her head. 'You do it.'

John plunged his hand into the hole he had made and felt around. In a moment he pulled out what looked like a small clod of dirt. Dangling from it was a dirty cord.

'What is it?' Candy whispered.

John worked at the crust of dirt with his thumbs and finally held the object out for Candy to see.

It was a watch and chain.

7

HEATHER COMES AGAIN

'GEE-MONEY,' said Huggy, 'hand that thing over again, will you? Why would there be a watch and chain under all that dirt? It's real old-fashioned, too. My grandpop's got one something like it.'

They were under an oak tree at the edge of the clearing, finishing the sandwiches and lemonade they had brought with them. Ellen had cleaned the watch and chain as best she could, but it was still speckly with dirt. The face under the crystal was pitted with rust, and the stem wouldn't wind, even though they had carefully cleaned away the clogging earth. But the case was almost certainly gold, and the chain as well.

'Gosh,' Huggy went on, 'if I left my Mickey Mouse watch under three *tons* of dirt, I'd go digging it out, and here's this expensive one under a few measly bucketfuls, and nobody even looks for it. It doesn't make sense.'

Ellen divided the last of the lemonade among the four plastic cups. 'It all gets peculiarer and peculiarer. There's Heather. Why hasn't she come around all day? Do you suppose Uncle Guy found out she'd crawled out of the window? And why does he watch her so closely, anyway? Why tell her there're rattlesnakes in the woods?'

'To keep her out of them,' Candy said promptly, forgetting that she hadn't intended to talk at all.

'Well of course, goofball,' Huggy said scornfully. 'But *why*?'

Candy was drawn in, in spite of herself. 'Because—because Uncle Guy doesn't want her talking to anybody because—because he's doing something wicked and she knows something.'

Huggy took off his glasses and rubbed them against his T-shirt, which only smeared them more. 'Now honest! You've been reading too many comic books. How could she talk to anybody else in the *woods*, for gosh sakes? John says nobody can get into the grounds if they're not wanted.'

'She talked to *us*, didn't she?' demanded Candy.

'That's true,' Ellen said. 'For heaven's sake, Huggy, you can be *fair*, even if—' She stopped short and there was an uncomfortable silence. They all avoided looking at Candy.

Candy stood up. 'You kids are just plain *mean*. I'm sick of being treated like a—a leper. I've been as nice as can be all day, and did my share of work and never grumbled or anything. I really tried *hard*, but you won't let me be friends. Well, I'm going straight back to the house and call up my father to come and get me. You can dig out your old tunnel, see if I care.' She stamped her foot. 'I'm *sorry* I said that stuff yesterday. I didn't really *mean* any of it. If you had any 'telligence you'd *know*.' She glared at them.

'Okay.' John suddenly grinned. 'All is forgave. Guess we've been sort of touchy with all this hard work, so we're sorry too.'

'Yup,' Huggy chimed in. 'You can't go off and leave us, just when everything's got so exciting, Candy-Andy. Besides,' he added grudgingly, 'I guess you're a pretty good digger, though it hurts muh right down here to say it.' He clasped his stomach.

'Everything hurts you there,' Ellen said. 'Huggy's got no heart, only a stomach. You mustn't mind Huggy, Candy. Nobody else does.'

'Well I like that,' Huggy complained. 'Poor little innocent Pindar gets stabbed in the back every time.'

'You'll get worse than that if you don't get down in the tunnel and start shovelling,' threatened John. 'I'm going to sickle some more grass.'

'Okay, okay,' said Huggy. 'Though what good it will do us to dig through to the other end while those logs are blocking the entrance, *I* don't know. I wish that Heather Whatshername would get on the ball.' He disappeared into the log cabin.

Ellen smiled at Candy. 'You won't go home, will you? We want you to stay. I'm sorry about leaving that note on my bed yesterday.'

'Oh, that's all right,' Candy said. She swallowed. 'I guess . . . I guess I just didn't think—'

'Hsst!' said Huggy, poking his head around the door of

the cabin. 'She's here. Come a-runnin'!' He disappeared inside again.

Ellen and Candy and John looked at each other and back at the cabin.

'He means Heather!' John exclaimed. 'Let's go.'

They scrambled pell-mell down the hole into the tunnel, Addle close behind. At first they couldn't see anything after the bright sunlight, but then they made out a glimmer of light coming from the far end. The candle had disappeared and Huggy was nowhere in sight.

'Where are you?' Ellen whispered.

'Over here,' said Huggy, his voice echoing loud in the tunnel. 'At the other end. I came over the top, but don't you try it—I bumped the ceiling on my way over and got a shower of dirt in my whiskers. You'll have to dig me out.'

They looked up at the gaping hole in the ceiling where several planks were missing just above the cave-in. Fresh dirt had fallen on top of the pile they had been shovelling out. It had extinguished the candle.

'All right,' John called back. 'Is Heather still there?'

'*He*llo,' she answered promptly. 'Are you all right?'

'Yes,' said Ellen. 'But what about you? We've been so worried all day . . .'

'Oh, I'm all right. Uncle Guy hasn't been home since morning, and Auntie Ruth is easy to fool.'

'Who is Auntie Ruth?' demanded Huggy.

Heather laughed. 'Uncle Guy's wife. She wears the most extraordin'ry high heels and furs and earrings and things. Uncle Martin absolutely *shudders* when he looks at her.'

Candy squeezed Ellen's arm in excitement.

'Listen,' John went on, 'do you have an Aunt Lib?'

'Aunt Who?'

'Lib. L-I-B.'

'Oh.' There was a short silence. 'Uncle Martin talks about an Aunt *Libby*, but I've never seen her. Uncle Martin's a darling. I do so wish Uncle Guy and Auntie Ruth would move back to town. They're so *bossy*. They won't let Uncle Martin invite any children here for tea, or *anything*. I wish I hadn't come to America at all, it's so beastly being all alone.'

'Why *did* you come?' Ellen asked.

'Kind Uncle Martin invited me when he was in England last summer. He's some sort of cousin, really. Mummy and Daddy simply adore him. It's only Uncle Guy who makes it beastly, and Auntie Ruth.'

'You ought to write to your mother and tell her,' Candy said indignantly.

'But then they would worry, and they're off in South Africa on Daddy's business for six months. That's why I came to visit Uncle Martin in the first place.'

'But can't Uncle Martin—' John began.

'Uncle Guy bullies him, rather, he's so gentle and sweet—' Heather broke off. 'Look here, I must go back now. Uncle Guy will be home soon and the first thing he'll ask is, "Where is Heather?" '

'We looked up Uncle Guy in the phone book,' John said, 'but the only Guy Howard lives in Capitol City. Is that your uncle?'

'Oh yes. He moved out to Howard Hall the day after I arrived. He said he wanted to know me better. Hateful old thing. I *must* go. I crawled out of the window again while Auntie Ruth was bathing. Huggy told me all of your names, so now I can think about you.' Her voice was wistful. 'I wish I could see you, too.'

'Did you move any of those logs?' John called.

'Yes, but not many, and I can't stay any longer. I'm

F

terribly sorry. I'll try to come back tomorrow. Why don't you bring a ladder? Then you could come over and help.'

'Okay,' said Huggy. 'We'll do 'er for sure.'

Heather laughed. 'You all sound so very *American*! I must fly. G'bye, Candy and Ellen and Huggy and John!'

''Bye, Heather,' they chorused.

They could hear her retreating footsteps for a few moments, and then all was still.

'Wow,' said John. 'Let's get out in the air where we can breathe.'

'Hey, what about *me*?' Huggy yelled.

'Oh my goodness, we've got to dig Huggy out.' Ellen grabbed the trowel. 'If he tries to come over the pile, he might hit the ceiling and bring down another avalanche.'

'Buried alive,' Huggy said with gloomy relish. 'I hope the rest of the ceiling's solid.'

John was inspecting the walls and roof of the tunnel. 'Hey, Huggy, pass the flashlight over. I want to see something.'

Candy stood back helplessly and watched. There wasn't room for more than one to dig at a time, and John was blocking the way out. He took the flashlight which Huggy slid over the dirt pile and shone its weakening light on the boards.

'What is it?' Candy asked anxiously after he had stood there for a few moments, whistling under his breath.

'Just figuring out how the thing could have caved in, in the first place. It's narrower here, but that wouldn't make any difference.' He scratched his head with the hand that held the torch, and the light played crazily over the tunnel. 'See, the side boards are sunk into the floor, and the top ones are fastened on with big metal braces. Good strong braces, too.'

'Maybe the wood rotted,' Ellen suggested, pausing for a moment in her digging.

'That's right,' Huggy said with mock bitterness, 'why don't you all sit around and have a nice cosy chat? It's only *me* over here. Hardly worth bothering about.'

'Shut up, Huggy, and take a look at the boards on your side,' John ordered.

'Sure, sure. But it just so happens that I left my special flashlight eyes in my other pocket. Wait a mo—I've got a match.'

There was a scratching sound, and then light flared up in the other end of the tunnel. 'Looks all right to me,' Huggy said. 'I know it's asking a lot of you, but would you mind getting on with the digging—that is, if you don't have anything better to do, of course.'

John took over the trowel from Ellen, who had found the candle and lit it, and then Candy had a turn. At last the dirt pile was low enough to allow Huggy to crawl over it. This he did gingerly, making himself as flat as possible. When he was on solid ground again, he shook himself.

'Remind me never to take a mining job,' he said. 'Every second on that pile, my hair was standing on end. All I could think of was that big old stone wall falling in and making one large-sized pancake of Pindar. Way I figure it, the wall's just about above that spot. Br-r-r, let's talk about something else.'

'You know . . .' said John, and then remained staring fixedly at the dirt heap.

'Know what?'

'Nothing.' John picked up the trowel. 'The rest of you go up top. I'm going to dig some more.'

When they gathered in the drawing-room after dinner that

night, Ellen said, 'I just can't *bear* to work on that code again. I'm so tired I could go to sleep standing on one leg.'

'Me too,' Huggy agreed. 'And we've still got to dig out the rest of the cave-in tomorrow, and build a new roof over it, and move all the logs at the other end and dig *that* end out . . . Woof! Makes me tired just to think about it!' He put his chin in his hands and stared emptily into space.

John gave an enormous yawn. 'I'm counting on finding the old boards at the bottom of the pile. That'll save a lot of time.'

Candy was horrified. 'You're not going to put the same ones up again! They might fall in!'

'We'll see,' John said wisely. 'I won't use them if they're not safe. You just trust Uncle John.'

Huggy sat up with a jerk and snapped his fingers. 'Be back in a minute,' he said, and dashed out of the room.

In a few moments he came bursting through the door again. 'Where's your knife, John, quick!' He pulled the gold watch and chain from his pocket and planted it on the table.

'What's the idea?' John asked, reaching for his scout knife.

'You'll see in a tick—if I'm right, that is.' He fumbled at the knife, and got the smallest blade open. 'I just remembered about my grandpop's watch, see? It's—here, you open it, John. I'm all thumbs.'

John took the watch and the knife from him. 'Take the crystal off, you mean?'

'No, no.' Huggy began to dance with excitement. 'The back of it. You can see the little groove-thing where you're supposed to open it with your thumbnail, only it's rusted shut or something. Well, not rusted, but—go on and open it, hurry *yup*!'

Frowning, John examined the back of the watch until he had located the groove. Then, slipping the point of the knife in, he pried gently. With a protesting rasp, the back of the case lifted away from the body of the watch on a hinge.

'If it's like my grandpop's,' said Huggy breathlessly, 'it'll have a name engraved on it. My grandpop said people always used to have their names engraved on their watches.'

There was a name engraved on this one, and a date:

Lowell Summer
1920

8

UG IN HGS TA KS OO LTM UC H

JOHN WAS the first to find his voice. 'Well, now we know something more about the cave-in. It couldn't have happened before 1920.'

'Huh?' Huggins looked up in bewilderment. 'Oh, I get it. You mean, if the watch is dated 1920 and it was under the dirt pile . . . yeah . . . sure. But how did it get there? Did the others hide it—gosh, that Uncle Guy was prob'ly a stinker even then!'

'I've got a hunch that the owner of the watch was wearing it when the cave-in happened,' said John quietly.

Ellen's hand flew to her mouth. 'The accident! Mr. Summer's weak back! Oh, John, it *must* have been the cave-in. Golly, though, he was lucky to get out at all! But—' She wrinkled her brow in thought. 'Oh dear, we're just guessing. I wish we *knew*!'

'Read all about it in the diary,' Huggy suggested mournfully.

'Good idea,' said John. 'In fact, I'm going to have another shot at it right now. Maybe we can get the rest of the pages open.'

'I'll help,' said Ellen. She went to the bookshelves and fished Low's journal out from its hiding place behind the other books.

With a concert of weary sighs, they gathered around the coffee table once more while John opened the book.

'I've been over it so much,' he said, 'that it almost makes sense the way it is. Listen. "Od yw tae ma ep an dls fo ou se . . ." '

'Sure, uh-huh,' Huggy nodded. 'Just what I was saying a minute ago.'

John leafed the pages over carefully. They looked at the diagrams of Howard Hall again. One good thing about them, John pointed out, was that if they ever got into Howard Hall, they could find their way around without any trouble. He leafed on. The pages at the back were still stuck together, but with a little prying, they separated. More pages of closely-printed code.

'The printing is better towards the end,' Ellen pointed out. 'Not so blocky. You would almost think it was written by a different person.'

'Hmm.' John examined closely the last pages of the diary and then turned back to the beginning to inspect 'OD YW TAE' again. 'Nope.' He traced a finger down the page.

'The G's are made the same way. Look. See the little squiggle on the bar? He does that in the last pages too.'

'Then he's just learned to write better between the beginning and the end,' said Candy. 'It's like in school. When you're in the third grade, your second grade writing looks like a baby's.'

'Mine looks like a giraffe's,' stated Huggy.

'Well, there's nothing here,' said John with a sigh of discouragement. 'No clues to the code. I move that we all go to bed.'

'Second the motion,' said Huggy. 'All those in favour, yawn.'

They all yawned and went upstairs.

'Off again for the woods?' Mrs. Addams asked them the next morning as they finished washing the dishes.

'Yep,' said John. 'You want me for something, Mom?'

'No, dear.' Mrs. Addams hung a tea towel over the rack, and then turned to look her son squarely in the eye. 'You *will* be careful, won't you? And sensible?'

John grinned. 'Sure, Mom. That's my middle name.'

'*Bien.* Go along then, children.'

'*Au 'voir*, Mom.'

'Were you speaking *French*?' Candy demanded as they set off through the woods.

'Yeah. Mom's half-Frog. Didn't you know?'

'She's *what*?'

'Half-French. So she's always at me to learn it.'

'Goodness.' Candy looked up at him, impressed. 'Say something in French.'

'Nah.'

'Please, John.'

'All right. *Tu es très jolie.*'

'Oh.' She said it over to herself. 'What does that mean?'

His funny eyebrows went up higher in the middle. 'That would be telling. Let's hurry up—we're getting left behind. Come on, Addle, pick up your big feet, boy.'

Addle barked and ran in circles around them until they caught up with the others.

The dirt pile in the tunnel looked discouragingly big when they started to work on it, but before very long Huggy, who was taking his turn with the trowel, stuck his head out of the cabin to announce that he had uncovered some old boards near the bottom of the heap.

'That's what I want to see,' said John. He propped the sickle against the cabin and followed Huggy into the tunnel. Candy and Ellen were close on his heels.

'Did you find the braces?' John asked.

'Haven't looked,' said Huggy. 'I just got down as far as the boards and came a-runnin'.'

The fat candles stuck into the dirt heap guttered and flared and threw their shadows big on the wall. John knelt and began tugging at the boards. 'Trowel,' he grunted. Huggy silently passed it over.

'Do hurry,' said Candy. 'I can't wait.'

'Sh-h-h,' Ellen silenced her.

With the trowel as a lever, John finally got the planks up from their bed of earth and stacked along the side. There were six of them, great thick pieces. John began probing at the tightly packed soil beneath. After long minutes he sat back and mopped at his forehead.

'I don't think there are any braces here,' he said in a queer voice. 'I think somebody removed them.'

'How could they remove them from under all that dirt?' Huggy asked. 'Doesn't make sense.'

'I mean they removed them *before* there was any cave-in.'

'On purpose?' Candy gasped.

'Well,' said John dryly, 'it'd be pretty hard to do it by accident. They were all screwed on with big heavy screws.'

They all stared silently at the dark gap in the roof. Candy's back suddenly felt crawly.

'Look there.' John pointed past the gap in the roof to the next set of planks. The top one rested on the sides, but it overlapped only slightly. 'You take those braces off, and it's just a matter of time till the roof falls in.' He shook his head disapprovingly. 'Not very good building. They should've cut their top boards longer.'

'That Unkie Guy sure was a nice feller,' said Huggy darkly.

'But he couldn't have known it would fall on *top* of Low,' Ellen said. 'Not unless Low sat right in that spot for twenty-four hours a day. Which he wouldn't. So it was just bad luck that the roof fell in when Low happened to be in the tunnel.'

'That's right,' John said thoughtfully. 'The way it could've happened was, Guy took the braces off for a sort of practical joke, and Low went hurrying through and bumped the sides by accident—it's awfully narrow right here.'

'Some practical joke,' said Huggy. 'I got whaled once for playing a practical joke. No wonder!'

'Well,' Ellen said with a shiver, 'what do you say we get on with the job? But you fix those boards good and tight, John Addams. We don't want to get socked on the head by the roof every time we go through the tunnel.'

'Sure, sure,' John nodded. 'It'll be duck soup. Trust yours truly.'

'Now who's beating his chest?' Candy said loftily.

John delivered a low bow in her direction, but when

ie straightened up, he cracked his head on the ceiling.
'Ouch!'

'Serves you right,' Candy said, but she laughed.

John and Huggy decided that some of the old planks
were strong enough to use again, but the two ceiling pieces
needed replacing. They crawled around the tunnel, measur-
ing and figuring and making scrawly notes in John's notebook. Huggy said he was sure he had seen some old braces
in the tool shed that looked the same size as those in the
tunnel.

Candy and Ellen watched the boys for a while until Huggy
complained that they were using up too much oxygen and
would they please move their carcases upstairs. They went
grumblingly, but Candy was secretly pleased to be out of
the damp tunnel. It wasn't very exciting standing around
while other people were having all the fun of doing the job.

'I wish—' Candy began when they had pulled themselves
out of the tunnel into the log cabin.

'You wish what?' Ellen asked.

'Oh nothing, I guess.' Candy wasn't really sure what she
had been going to say, except that she suddenly felt, as they
emerged into daylight, that she was enjoying herself with
these kids, that she almost felt as though she actually
belonged. It was hard to explain. 'I just wish we could figure
out the code, don't you?'

'Sure do.' Ellen wiped her hands on her jeans and opened
the door. Addle, who had been kept out of the tunnel,
rushed joyfully up to them, his black ears flopping. He
pranced around them, and then, seeing the door open behind them, made for it.

'Oh no you don't, little dog,' said Ellen, and collared him
while Candy pushed the door shut. 'Poor Addle. He found

the tunnel first of all, and now we've taken it away from him
and won't even let him in. It's not fair, is it, Addle?'

But Addle, released again, only went careening around
them as though he was completely happy.

'He doesn't care,' said Candy, laughing. 'Maybe he thinks
it's just a game.' She glanced back at Ellen, who was staring
at the cabin door. 'What's the matter?'

'Come here,' Ellen said, almost in a whisper. 'I think—
Listen, just take a quick look at this lettering and see if it
doesn't sort of make words.'

Candy looked puzzledly at the carved-out letters on the
door.

ND RG UER OU DS AT NTI ON 2

1915

LIB   GUY
LOW   MART

Finally, she shook her head. 'I don't see—'

'Then read it out,' Ellen said, clasping her shoulder
excitedly.

Candy looked helplessly at the letters. ' "N-D-R-G—" '
she began.

'No, not that way. Read the *sounds*. You have to sort of
put in some vowels to help out, but—'

'Wait, I see!' Candy's eyes sparkled. 'UND-ERG-OO-
ROUD. Ellen, it's UNDERGROUND! But what's the rest
of it? SAT-N-SHUN 2. Sat-n-shun, Sat-n-shun . . . I
don't . . .'

'Just look at it a minute,' Ellen said anxiously. 'Couldn't it
be STATION? UNDERGROUND STATION 2?'

'Golly!' Candy breathed. 'You *did* it, Ellen! You did it!
You broke the code!'

'Well, not exactly. I mean, I just happened to look at the

thing right, and there it was. Anybody could do that if they'd looked.'

Candy stared at her in astonishment. 'Why, Ellen Vance, they could not! You're—you're terribly smart! I'm going to tell the boys.' She flung open the door and shouted down the tunnel. 'Hey, come on out quick! Ellen's broken the code!'

'What?' came John's hollow voice.

'She said Ellen's busted something,' Huggy said. 'Sounded like her *toe*. We better go see.'

They came scrambling out a moment later, looking around anxiously.

'What happened?' John asked. 'Did Ellen hurt her toe?'

'The code!' Candy said. 'Not her toe, silly. Ellen's broken the *code*. She can read what's on the door.'

Ellen's calm voice penetrated through Addle's excited barking. 'I haven't *really* broken it, but I think we might be able to figure out how it's done now. Come on out and look.'

They clustered around the door to examine the letters while Ellen explained how she had stumbled on to the solution.

'By gummy,' said Huggins, 'why, it's plain as John's red nose. And we never even saw it! Boyohboy, I can't wait to get my paws on that diary!' He rubbed his hands together eagerly.

John was already writing the letters down in his notebook. 'This does it, all right,' he said with a grin that went all over his face. He tore the page out and handed it to Ellen. 'That is, as soon as you've figured out how the code works, you and Candy. Come on, Hug, back to the salt mines for us.'

'Aw, hey,' Huggy protested, 'aren't we all going to work on the code?' He pushed his glasses up higher on his nose and looked miserably at the sheet of paper in Ellen's hand.

'I need help,' John said briefly.

'Aw right.' Huggy gave a last despairing look at the paper and started to follow John into the cabin.

'*I'll* help John,' Candy suddenly heard herself saying.

Huggy whirled around and stared at her unbelievingly. 'Yuh *mean* it?'

Candy shrugged. 'I just hate twiddling around with bitsy pieces of paper.'

'You must be bats.' Huggy beamed. 'But thanks, pal. You can come to my next three birthday parties. Wow! Let's see that paper, Ellen.' He began grubbing in his pockets for a pencil.

'Nice of you,' John said gruffly when he and Candy had clambered into the tunnel. 'Letting old Hug work on the code.'

'Oh . . . well . . .' Candy didn't quite know what to say. She really hadn't wanted to work on the dry old code, or she wouldn't have traded jobs with Huggy. But a warm little glow of pleasure started up inside her at John's praise. She almost wished she was crazy about codes and had given over to Huggy just to be nice.

Mrs. Summer had gone in to Capitol City on business again, so the children could talk about the code and the tunnel at lunchtime. Otherwise, as Huggy said, they would have busted themselves trying to keep quiet. Ellen, with many interruptions from Huggy, explained what they had done about breaking the code. It was harder than it looked at first because they didn't know exactly how to take hold of the problem. Huggy produced a wadded heap of paper and began to smooth them out on the tablecloth.

'What we fine'ly did,' he broke in, 'was write out UNDERGROUNDSTATION all together—well, I guess it was really Ellen's idea—and then we went through and drew

oxes around the letters that were on the door, see? Like
ND and RG, and so on. Looky here.' He handed a dog-
ared sheet across the table to Candy and John.

U|ND|E|RG|R|OU|N|DS|T|AT|I|ON|

'Then it was easy, wasn't it, Ellen?'
'Well, yes, when we caught on that the groups of three
etters were a sort of *collection* of letters—the ones that got
eft out of the boxes—'
'Yeah,' Huggy went on quickly. 'You take *Huggins*, f'r'in-
tance. It turns out to be UG IN HGS. Then if you wanted to
ay "Huggins is a clever boy"—'
John, who had been working over his notebook, tore out
sheet and put it in the middle of the table. Is this the idea?'
e asked innocently.
On the paper he had printed:

UG IN HGS TA KS OO LTM UC H

Huggy leaned over eagerly to read it. 'I'll bet I can decode
t without even using a pencil. Listen. "Huggins . . . um
. . talks . . . too . . . uh . . ." Hey! That's a dirty
rick!'

9

TWO UNCLES OVERHEARD

Mrs. Addams wouldn't let them wash the dishes—'No
on such a sunshiny day,' she said—so Candy and Elle
gathered up the diary, two old bits of candle, paper an
pencils, and helped Mrs. Addams pack sandwiches an
lemonade in a basket, while the boys went out to the too
house. Fifteen minutes later they all met in the play yard
John's and Huggy's hip pockets bristled with hammer
screwdrivers, metal braces of various sizes, screws and nails
A long ladder, two thick boards and a saw were lying on th
grass. Standing over them was Mr. Jacobs, the gardene
and handyman, looking thunderous.

'Aw, we just want to borrow the tools, Mr. Jake,' Huggy said. 'We'll bring them back, honest.'

'Like you brung back the spade?' Mr. Jacobs asked caustically. His bushy eyebrows were like a prickly hedge over his thin brown face. '*An*' the trowel. *An*' the sickle. What if I jest step up to the house and inform Miz Summer what's going on here?'

'But we're *using* the spade and trowel and sickle,' John protested, 'and they're not your best ones. Besides, you know we always bring things back, Mr. Jake—in the end.'

'In the end!' Mr. Jacobs spluttered. '*Which* end, I wanta know. The end of summer? And how am I supposed to get on with my work? Ever' time I go to the tool shed, somethings else turns up missing. Next thing you'll be taking joy rides on the power mower.' He gave a snorting sort of laugh. 'Now you jest march this stuff right back to where you got it—'

'Oh, Mr. Jake . . .' Ellen wailed.

Candy stamped her foot. 'You mean old thing!'

'S-s-ssh,' said John, but Candy went right on, her face pink with anger.

'I don't care! You're an old spoilsport, that's what you are. I'll bet nobody in the whole world likes you, Mr. Jacobs!'

Mr. Jacobs scowled at her, his face settling like granite into its deep seams. 'An' how many friends *you* got—with a tongue like that? Your ma oughta spank you, that's what. I've half a mind to do it myself.'

'Oh please don't pay any attention to Candy,' Ellen pleaded. 'She doesn't mean to be impolite.'

'I do too,' Candy began, but John stepped on her foot.

'We-ell . . . ' Mr. Jacobs's face softened when he looked at Ellen. 'Tell you what, young lady. I'll lend the stuff to

G

you, being's you're always sech a dependable one. But mind
you bring everything back or I'll put a lock on the tool shed
and nobody'll git *nothing*!' He divided a glare amongst the
other three and then turned and stumped off.

'Thank you, Mr. Jake,' they chorused after him, but he
gave no sign of hearing them.

'Why,' Candy said indignantly, 'I'll bet he meant to let
us have the tools all the time!'

'Of course he did,' Ellen said. 'It's a sort of game. He's
awfully disappointed if you don't play up.' She looked
reflectively at Candy. 'You hurt his feelings, talking like
that.'

Candy's eyes flew wide. 'Well, I *thought* he was just being
mean!'

'All the same,' Ellen said gently, 'you made him feel bad.
Now he'll grumble at the asparagus beds all morning and
won't go up to the kitchen for his morning coffee.'

'Oh.' Candy stood stockstill.

'Hurry *yup*, you guys,' called Huggy. He and John had
hoisted the ladder off the ground. 'We're all set.'

Without a word, Candy whirled and ran off in the direction Mr. Jacobs had gone. She found him on his knees in
the vegetable garden, inspecting a tomato plant.

'I'm sorry, Mr. Jacobs,' she gasped out all in one breath.
'I don't think you're a spoilsport at all and I'm sorry I said
it.'

'Uh?' Mr. Jacobs grunted. He didn't look around, but
his back straightened. 'Ne'mind, little girl. We all make
mistakes. Bein' sorry for them's a good thing, but it's better
when you don't have to spend your hull life apollygizing.
Run along, now.'

'Yes, well . . . well, good-bye, Mr. Jake.'

Mr. Jacobs lifted a knobby hand in farewell and Candy

ran back to the play yard, feeling suddenly much lighter. The others didn't ask any questions about her running off, but John silently gave her an end of the ladder to carry while Huggy took the other end, and Ellen and John loaded up with the two heavy planks and the saw. They started off.

Addle went wild with excitement when he saw the ladder moving along. He barked fiercely at the rungs, then raced round and round, and finally jumped through, almost knocking the ladder out of Candy's and Huggy's hands.

'Hey! Whoa! Stop it!' Huggy yelled. But round and round Addle tore, ears laid back and eyes wild. Then phlap! he leaped through the ladder.

'He'll soon get tired and stop,' Ellen consoled.

'So'll I,' threatened Huggy. 'Addle! Settle down, you. For gosh sakes, somebody give him a cucumber sandwich.'

When at length they got to the log cabin, Ellen and Huggy settled down in the grass to work at the diary, while Candy and John lugged the boards and tools into the tunnel. They had decided to finish the inside of the tunnel before going over the wall on the ladder to clear away the pile of logs Heather had talked about. 'First things first,' as John said. Besides, they were all eager to know what Lowell Summer's 'Private Journal' contained. So Huggy and Ellen scribbled and muttered and mumbled over the coded words in the mouldy old book, and John and Candy lifted and tugged boards and drove screws in the dank air of the underground passage. Candy was frightened at first of another cave-in, but John worked carefully and slowly, and when they raised the boards into position, only a little dirt sifted down on them.

In the middle of operations, Huggy lowered himself head first into the tunnel entrance like a nuthatch and announced triumphantly that he and Ellen had decoded the first page of the diary. He passed in a crumpled sheet of paper, which Candy and John read by the light of the flickering candle.

> Today we made plans for our secret underground railway. Exactly six feet from the wall on the Howard side we will begin to dig. Each one will work at digging for fifteen minutes at a time while the others start building the first station. Lib and I think we should ask Maxwell to help, but Guy says we can do it ourselves. At first Martin was on our side, and then he changed to Guy's. He always does what Guy says. But Lib never does. This is the first diary I ever kept. Today is May seventh. No more lessons because Old Tinderbox fell down the stairs and broke his collarbone. He said that Guy tripped him, but Mr. Howard did not believe it and dismissed him. I told Mother that Guy probably did, but she said Old Tin had another position anyway and would not suffer. We all go away to school next fall except Lib.

They talked excitedly about the entry while they went on with the work of rebuilding the tunnel. John thought that Old Tinderbox must have been a tutor for the children and probably lived at Howard Hall while he taught Guy and Martin and Lib and Lowell. Lowell would go around to Howard Hall every day for his lessons. Maybe the long trip around to the gate gave them the idea for building the tunnel.

About four o'clock the new boards were firmly anchored in place. John yelled for Ellen and Huggy, who came tumbling down to join them, Addle at their heels. John carried the candle and they advanced cautiously to the other end of the tunnel. A small amount of light flickered through the opening, but leaves and earth had sifted in and clogged all but a small section of the entrance.

'More digging,' Huggy groaned. 'Oh my aching back!'

'Easier though,' said John. 'The ground's looser. Besides, Addle's already done a lot of the digging for us, getting in and out.'

'Sh-h,' cautioned Ellen. 'What's that?'

They all stood motionless, heads bowed beneath the low roof. There was a crackling sound as of somebody walking near them.

'It's Heather,' Candy exclaimed, but Huggy clapped his hand over her mouth. Addle whined softly. The footsteps stopped.

'What was that?' a man's voice demanded harshly. Candy shook her head free from Huggy's clasp and sank to the ground beside Addle. He crept closer to her, shivering. John blew out the candle.

'I didn't hear anything, Guy.' The other voice was gentle, and a little sad.

'You never do,' the first one grated. 'The kid goes jumping out of windows all over the place and you don't know anything about it, do you?'

This was Uncle Guy, Candy realized with a shiver, and he was talking to Uncle Martin about Heather. She huddled closer to Addle.

'But you can't expect to keep a child penned up, Guy. She only wanted to exercise her legs a bit. What harm is there in that?'

'Don't be a fool. You know our dear neighbour is just sitting over there in Summer House waiting for a chance to even the score. If she ever got hold of Heather, she'd never stop until she knew everything that was going on over here.'

The children clutched each other. He was talking about Mrs. Summer!

'But Heather doesn't know anything,' the gentle voice protested.

'She knows she's locked out of your studio and that you're painting something for me. How long do you think it would take our dear neighbour to put two and two together? No, Martin, you just keep on with your paint brushes, and I'll handle Heather.'

There was a sudden loud plunking sound just over the children's heads. They huddled closer together, scarcely breathing.

'It looks all right,' the grating voice said. 'Tumbled around a bit, though.' Again the plunking sound, as though he was kicking a log. '*She* could have moved them. I don't suppose you were insane enough to tell her about the old tunnel, were you?'

'No, no,' the other said. 'Of course not. And the way the logs are tumbled around, Guy—I tried to shift them one day a few years back. Thought I'd like to see if the hole is still there. Too much for me, though. I had to give it up.'

'No fool like an old fool,' Guy said roughly. 'Well, that's that. Let's get back to the house. You need these daylight hours to finish. You've only got until Friday night.'

'Guy—' Martin's voice started hesitantly and then became firm. 'When I've finished the painting, you're going to let us alone. You and Ruth will move back to Capitol City and—'

Guy laughed. It wasn't a pleasant laugh. 'Come now, you're not going to try to throw me out of my own house, are you? Have you forgotten that I own this fine crumbling mansion and that you haven't one cent to spend unless I give it to you? Besides, if all goes well, I might have another job for you soon.'

'No!' Martin's voice was so loud that the children

jumped. 'No, Guy, this is the end! I wouldn't have done this one if I hadn't been afraid for the child!'

'You'll do as I say,' Guy replied. 'You always have, and you always will.'

'That's where you're wrong,' said Martin, so softly that the children only just heard him. Candy could feel her skin prickling with excitement at the dead earnestness of his voice.

Even Guy seemed taken aback. 'We've wasted enough of the daylight here,' he muttered. 'Let's go.'

Their footsteps receded, but long after they had faded away, the children crouched in the tunnel without a sound except for their breathing and Addle's panting.

At long last, John stirred. 'Let's get out of here,' he whispered. 'I won't light the candle. We'll just have to grope along.'

Outside, on the grass, they looked at each other with scared faces.

'What should we do?' Ellen whispered.

'Do?' repeated John. 'Why, we go over the wall and move those logs first of all and get our tunnel finished. We can't keep hauling this ladder around.'

'Then we'll go find Heather and sneak her out of Howard Hall,' said Huggins, happily circling the rims of his glasses.

'*I* think we should tell Mrs. Summer and get the police,' said Candy determinedly. 'And I'm going to do it if you don't, so there!'

Huggins gritted his teeth. 'If you do, I'll—I'll put frogs in your bed.'

'I don't care. There's something awful going on, and that Uncle Guy *is* doing something bad, and we're only kids . . .'

'All right,' said John. 'And what would you tell the police?'

'Why—why—' Candy was taken by surprise. 'Well, I'd tell them what we heard today and—'

'Sure,' said John, 'but when you tell about things, they never sound the way they really happened, especially to grown-ups. Anyway, we don't really *know* anything. We've just been guessing. The police can't go sticking their noses into people's business because somebody only guesses something. They've got to have a little proof.'

'Well, but—'

'Besides all that,' John went on, 'wait till you hear who Uncle Guy Howard is. I just up and asked Mr. Jake this noon, casual-like—that's what brought him down on our heads—and then in all the excitement over the tools, I clean forgot about it. Anyway, Uncle Guy only owns the Modern Art Institute in Capitol City, that's all. Well, a lot of rich people own it now, really—a sort of Society—but he's the curator or something and bosses the show. Heck, his father *started* the Institute. You think the police are going to believe anything you say about someone as important as that?'

'The Modern Art Institute!' Candy sat up straight. 'Why, my mother and father belong to that! They gave a thousand dollars to it just a little while ago. I know, because I saw the cheque. They give it every year.'

Huggy whistled. 'One thousand bucks! Wow! Imagine giving away one thousand bucks!' He rubbed at his glasses. 'I once gave a whole dollar to the polio fund, though, come to think of it.'

'Well, Mother and Daddy say that art is very important.' Candy felt a little embarrassed because they had also said you shouldn't talk about money. 'Besides, it's all abducted from income tax or something.'

John said seriously, 'I don't know what Uncle Guy's

doing with your Mom and Dad's thousand dollars, but something very odd is going on, and it has to do with painting.'

'Maybe he's buying Uncle Martin's paintings instead of real famous ones,' Ellen suggested. 'And keeping the money. Goodness, if all the members give a thousand dollars and there are, well, twenty members, that's twenty thousand dollars right there!'

They all stared at each other, boggling at such a sum.

'Well,' said Candy hotly, 'I think we ought to *do* something about it! Let's get started!'

'Huh,' muttered Huggy, 'you wanta get Candy innersted, you just wave dollar signs in front of her.'

'Shut up, Huggy,' John said sternly. 'Candy can't help being rich.'

They arranged that two should go up the ladder and over the wall, while the other two would dig out the tunnel from inside. Huggy declared that he was hot at log-lifting, but John said it was his turn inside the tunnel.

'I'll take Candy,' John said. 'She'll be good at camouflaging the entrance. We'll have to fix the logs so they won't look as though we'd moved them. Besides, Candy works hard.'

'When she gets started,' Huggy muttered. 'Ah, well, many a good man has begun at the bottom.'

John went up the ladder first and stepped off on to the thick stone wall. When Candy scrambled up, they both heaved at the ladder while Ellen and Huggy pushed from below. That was the hardest part—getting it up far enough to balance it on top of the wall. Then they could let it slide down the other side.

'Though we'll have to be careful,' John pointed out. 'If we drop it, we'll really be in a pickle.'

They let the ladder down gently. Candy was frightened

at being up so high, but she didn't dare say anything in front of John after he'd said that about camouflaging. So she tried not to look down, and hung on to her side of the ladder with all her strength.

Then it was in place and John climbed down and held it steady for Candy. They decided to lay the ladder in the tall weeds beside the wall where it wouldn't be easily seen if Uncle Guy should come back.

This side of the wall looked much the same as the Summer House side except that what had once been a log cabin play house was now only a disorderly pile of logs with a sagging door on top. The clearing was not so large as their own, and Candy had the shivery feeling that the great oaks and sycamores were threatening them. The woods looked denser and gloomier than the Summer woods.

'Let's get going,' John said in a whisper.

Maybe he was scared too, Candy thought, and she felt better. They took hold of the door that was lying on top of the pile and tugged it down off the heap. It made a lot of noise sliding over the logs, and Candy glanced fearfully over her shoulder at the woods. She half expected Uncle Guy to come running out. John was scraping at one of the boards in the door with his finger-nail.

'It's almost worn away,' he whispered, 'but it says the same thing our door does. Only it's Underground Station 1, instead of 2.'

'Yes,' said Candy, with another anxious glance at the woods. 'Let's hurry with the logs.'

In a few moments they heard a 'hist!' from the tunnel. Ellen and Huggy were at work with spade and trowel.

'The thing is,' said John, when they had at last moved all the logs that covered the hole, 'we've got to fix it so nobody can see the entrance but so we can get in and out easily.'

'And it mustn't look too different from the way it was—in case Uncle Guy comes back,' added Candy.

'I wish you kids would hurry up,' came Ellen's anxious whisper between thuds of the spade. 'You make me nervous out there.'

'We're making our own selves nervous—don't need your help,' John retorted. He rubbed his hand over his face, leaving streaks of dirt. 'Come on, Candy, let's criss-cross four logs with the hole in the middle for a start.'

They laid the logs out like a giant game of ticktacktoe, but Candy said it looked too regular and they should 'careless it up' a bit. So they angled the top logs out of the precise pattern.

'Hey,' Huggy complained, 'you're shooting more dirt down here. Let up!'

'Push the spade through,' John said, 'and I'll shoot lots more your way. It'll be easier digging from here.'

The handle of the spade appeared, and John drew it out. Candy danced with impatience while he shovelled the fairly pliable earth. The recent rain had softened the ground, and the spade bit into it easily.

'Take it easy!' Huggy yipped. 'You're filling up the hole and cutting off our air.'

'Then scoop a little faster,' said John cheerfully.

'Why don't you get mad at Huggy?' Candy asked suddenly. 'I mean the way you all do with me. He says rude things and complains all the time, but you just laugh.'

John leaned on the spade and looked intently at it. 'Huggy just likes to talk. He doesn't mean any of that stuff.'

'Well, but neither do I.' Candy could feel herself flushing. 'Not really. I just—'

'Then nobody'll get sore at you.' John went back to his digging.

Candy watched him, perplexed. These kids had a funny way of looking at things. Like John saying she couldn't help it if she was rich. As though being rich was like having an extra head or something. They didn't seem at all envious. Candy frowned thoughtfully.

Huggy's voice came out of the tunnel. 'Aw, go on discussing Huggins Pindar. Doesn't matter what you say as long as you go on talking about me.'

'Quiet, riot,' said John. 'You want to bring Uncle Guy running?'

Candy glanced apprehensively at the thickly growing trees. The sooner they got out of here, the better. She grabbed hold of a log and dragged it up on the crisscross. Thing was to pile as many logs in *front* of the entrance as possible. And they ought to fix it so the rain wouldn't go into the tunnel. The old door would make a good roof. She took hold of another log and tugged.

'Spade coming through,' John announced quietly, and thrust the handle into the hole. It was drawn down rapidly.

'T'anks, pal,' said Huggy. 'Us moles down here sure are grateful.'

Candy and John heaved log upon log, around and over the tunnel entrance. They left a space on the side nearest the wall for crawling in and out, and camouflaged it by leaning logs against the pile. Then, to put the door on top, they had to climb halfway up the pile. They had just got it into position when the log they were both standing on slipped, and sent them sliding down to the ground.

'What happened?' Ellen called. 'Are you all right?'

'Sure,' John groaned, trying to rub his elbows and shins at the same time. 'How about you, Candy?' Candy had scraped her back, but she was looking ruefully at a tear in her blouse. And three buttons had popped off the back of it. John took her hand and pulled her up.

'Hey, you really skinned your backbone. Doesn't that hurt?'

'Not much,' Candy said, feeling very brave. 'I'll bet we wrecked the pile, though.'

John darted around to the entrance and was back in a moment. 'Nope. It's swell. And look, what we did to this part makes it just right now. Pardner, shake!'

They solemnly shook hands. Candy felt a little thrill of excitement. They had finished their job, and she'd been brave about her hurt back—but best of all, she felt that John really was her friend.

OR CO MED E

'LISTEN TO THIS,' Huggy said suddenly. The children were gathered around the big coffee table in the drawing-room, but there was no fire tonight, for even Summer House, generally cool, was warm and close, as though a storm was on the way.

Huggy read from the sheet of code he had been working on:

'Today is the twentieth of May and Guy was digging in the tunnel when some of the roof fell on him. He blamed me because I was the last person to work on it yesterday. For once Martin took my part and of course Lib did too. She has found a book about tunnels that shows how to prevent cave-ins. We decided to ask Maxwell to help, but we made him swear that he would never tell anybody our secret. Lib and I promised him some of our pocket money every week, but Guy wouldn't give any of his and wouldn't let Martin, either, though Mart gave me some secretly. Guy says that my father pays Maxwell too much anyway.'

'It's just like Guy to blame somebody else!' Ellen exclaimed. 'And then to be so mean about poor Maxwell. You'd think the others would just tell him off.'

'They were afraid of him,' John said. 'Look what happened to Old Tinderbox, for instance. *He* got tossed down the stairs.'

'I've got something to read,' Candy announced. She had been working busily over the sheets assigned to her and found it rather fun, after all.

'Twenty-seventh of May. Dad noticed that the lumber pile is getting lower and asked what we were building. I said it was a secret and he only laughed and said Maxwell must be having a secret too because he was missing all afternoon yesterday and the roof wasn't mended yet. Then he said Maxwell was a good man for a building job and one couldn't do better, so that is all right. Max boarded up the sides and top of the tunnel as far as we've gone and showed us where to start digging on our side so we would finally meet in the middle. Lib is going to work with me on our side. Guy pretends he is afraid to dig anywhere around me for fear he will be caved-in on again. But it wasn't my fault. Lib says not to pay any attention to Guy, but some day I'm going to punch him in the nose, even if he is bigger.'

'I hope he does!' Ellen said. 'Uncle Guy is nothing but a big bully!'

They worked on in silence broken by mutterings and the scratch of pencils on paper. Then suddenly Ellen said, 'He's done it! Wait a minute, while I figure out the rest of this.' Several minutes went by with all of them bent over their work, and then Ellen settled back on her heels.

'A lot of this just tells about how much work they got done each day, and about Maxwell's brother coming to help dig, so I'll skip that part. But listen to this!

> 'June seventeenth. Today we broke through to where Guy and Martin had stopped digging. Guy was mad because Maxwell helped us, so he and Martin didn't come any farther than halfway, and they put up their own boards. Also they made the middle part narrower than the rest. I said Maxwell ought to do the boards over because the top ones were too short and we should widen the tunnel and then Guy said he'd rather do his own boarding to be sure it was safe because Maxwell couldn't be trusted any more than me. The next thing I knew I hit Guy in the nose and we had a fight right in the tunnel. It was lucky for me the tunnel wasn't bigger. Guy kept banging into the sides and the roof and I blacked both his eyes. I've just got one black eye. Maxwell was scared and made us stop, but I honestly won. We shook hands then, but Guy didn't much want to. We decided to leave the tunnel narrow in the middle, and Max said the boards would be safe enough when he puts braces on them. Guy's nose bled where I punched it.'

'Good *for* him, too,' said John. 'Too bad Maxwell pulled them apart. Low would have beat the stuffing out of Guy.'

'Well, now we know why the tunnel is narrower in the middle and why those top boards were short,' Huggy said. 'It was old Guy skimping on the work. Jiminy, let's hurry up and decode some more.'

They learned that the tunnel had finally been finished, complete with trapdoors at either end, on July first. On July second Lowell and Guy had an argument over the building of the first log cabin, which Guy and Martin had started, and Guy rolled stones over the Howard trapdoor to keep Lowell from coming over to that side of the wall. So Lib made the long trip around by the main gates to help Low build his cabin, and Maxwell and his brother pitched in as well. After that, they all seemed to become friends again, and the Howard log cabin was completed five days after the Summer cabin. For the rest of July and all of August they played at being escaped slaves going through the underground railway. It was at this time that Lowell made the diagrams of Howard Hall, as part of the game.

'Here's something,' John said. He was working a few pages beyond the last diagram.

> 'The third of September. This is our last week before we go off to our schools, except Lib. She is going to have a governess. Lib said if we each buried some possession in the same place we would always be friends and come back to that place. She read it in some book. We finally decided to bury our W-W's all together in a waterproof box, so that's what we did.'

'W-W's,' Huggy repeated. 'Wrist-watches? Hey, maybe they're still buried!'

'But doesn't it say *where* they buried them? The—the W-W's?' Candy asked.

'Nope.' John shook his head. 'And the next entry is Thanksgiving Day. They're all home from school for a week, that's all.' He flipped over a page. 'Wait a minute. I'm on to something else here. It's . . . let me see . . . it's after Christmas, this next page. AR IN MTF AI ED IS

LHE XA IN TI MAO NS . . . "Martin failed his examinations . . ." ' John began scribbling down words directly from the diary and reading them out as he went:

> 'Martin failed his examinations so he is going to stay home and learn to paint. That's what he wants to do. He painted a picture of our Christmas tree and gave it to me. Guy made fun of it but I think it is very, very good. Every single ornament is there—I counted them to see. I think Guy is jealous. He said Martin was a copycat, not a painter. I asked Dad, but he said you couldn't tell so early. He said really good artists have to put in something of themselves besides just painting what is there. I don't think I understand this.'

'Me, neither,' said Huggy, 'unless it means mixing a drop of your blood with the paint. *Then* you'd be putting something of yourself in it!'

'What I don't understand,' said Ellen with a puzzled frown, 'is how Uncle Guy can get away with it. I mean, it looks as if he's making Uncle Martin paint a picture for the Institute, doesn't it?'

The others nodded.

'Well, then, don't you think people like Candy's mother and father would kick up an awful fuss when they find out their money's been spent for a painting that's not much good?'

'We don't *know* whether it's any good or not,' John pointed out. 'Maybe Uncle Martin's a famous painter.'

'Yes, but there's a shady deal going on,' said Huggy. 'You heard the things Uncle Guy said this afternoon.'

'That's right,' Candy agreed. 'There's something funny about Uncle Guy *forcing* Uncle Martin to paint a picture for thousands of dollars.'

They looked at each other blankly. In the hall, the big clock chimed nine times. A moment later they heard Mrs. Summer's footsteps. When she came in, all the papers and the diary were safely tucked away, and the children were yawning over their books.

II

THE W-W'S

WHEN CANDY woke up the next morning, she still felt
excited, even though her back was sore where she
had scraped it on the logs. They had actually finished the
tunnel yesterday, or at least got it opened enough to crawl
through. And they had broken the code and read a great
deal of Low Summer's diary. And John had shaken her
hand and called her pardner. And he had said something to
her in French which she couldn't understand, but it sounded
nice. Ellen and Huggy had been different, too, she thought,
even though Huggy kept calling her nitwit and duck brain.
But he called the others that and they didn't seem to mind.

They just told him to shut his head and then grinned and that was that.

Candy wiggled her toes happily under the covers, but kept her eyes closed. Today they were going through the tunnel to the Howard side of the wall to find Heather and bring her back with them to talk to Mrs. Summer. They would tell the whole story then, and Mrs. Summer would know what to do . . .

Gradually, Candy became aware of a sound which she realized had been going on ever since she woke up. Her eyes flew open. Rain! Great slithering sheets of it against the windows.

'Oh no!' she cried out.

Ellen stirred, lifted her head sleepily from her pillow. 'What's the matter?' She sat upright. 'Not rain again! It's not *fair*!'

A faint rumble of thunder answered her from the distance.

After breakfast and chores, they gathered glumly in the drawing-room. The rain was pouring down as hard as ever, with no sign of letting up. Lightning flashed and thunder rolled outside the windows. John built the fire, Candy and Huggins got into an argument over Benjamin Franklin's experiments with lightning, and Ellen settled it by saying neither of them knew what he was talking about.

Mrs. Summer came in, wearing a mackintosh, to say that she and Mrs. Addams had an important appointment to keep in Capitol City, but Mrs. Norland, the cleaning woman, would be in the house to look after them.

'We're winding up our business affairs tomorrow,' she said with a smile. 'I hope you children haven't been bored, being on your own for so long. You can think up something special to do on Saturday as a sort of celebration. A movie or a swimming party or . . .'

'I like art galleries,' Candy said suddenly. 'Could we go to an art gallery maybe?'

Mrs. Summer stopped in the act of putting on her gloves. 'Why, yes, if you all want to. There's a special exhibition coming on, I believe. I'll have to look it up in the *News-Chronicle* when I get back. Well, is everything all right then? You won't go out while it's storming, of course?'

'No, we won't,' Huggy said, jiggling in his chair. 'You'd better not be late for your 'pointment, Mrs. S.'

They waited until they heard her car go down the drive and then made a dash for Mrs. Summer's study. The morning's *News-Chronicle* was on the desk. They all made a snatch for it, but John's agile fingers were first.

'Look on the Society page,' Ellen said. 'Where it says "Announcements" or "Calendar" or something.'

John got the paper open, spread it on the floor, and the others crowded around him. He leafed over a page. Ellen speared at a column with her forefinger. 'There. "Coming Events in Capitol City." What does it say?'

They scanned the column together:

> Friday, June 18. Capitol City Choir Concert, Municipal Auditorium, 8:15 p.m.
> Saturday, June 19. Opening of *Strong Box,* Little Theatre Group, Little Theatre, 8:30 p.m.
> Sunday, June 20. Exhibition of newly-acquired paintings, Modern Art Institute, 3:30 p.m.

'Newly-acquired paintings,' Ellen breathed. 'There it is.'

'But shouldn't it tell *what* the paintings are?' asked Candy. 'There ought to be a story about them somewhere in the paper.'

'Good idea,' John said. He turned the paper back to the front page and they began going through it, column by column. But there was no story on the Modern Art Institute.

Huggy jumped up and dashed for the door. 'Back in a sec,' he said.

When he returned, he was carrying a load of newspapers up to his nose. 'All the old ones I could find,' he gasped. 'Somebody grab them, quick!' With that, the top papers began to slide like an avalanche. A moment later *News-Chronicles* littered the rug all around him.

The others scrambled over the floor picking them up. Mrs. Norland, the cleaning woman, appeared in the doorway with vacuum cleaner and a basketful of attachments. She was almost as wide as she was tall, and her grey hair was trying to escape from an untidy knot at the back.

'Shoo. Scoot,' she said amiably. 'Git your truck together and git. There's them as has work to do; and them that hasn't, better disappear.' She stood over them until they had gathered up all the papers and carried them into the drawing-room.

Ellen divided the newspapers into four stacks and they all stretched out on the floor around the fire and began the search for a story about the Modern Art Institute. The rain still drummed steadily on the windows, but the thunder had died away to an occasional distant rumble.

After a while John looked over at Huggy, who was intent on his paper. 'It won't be on the comic page, Hug.'

'Huh? Oh.' Huggy looked sheepish and turned back to the Society page. 'I don't see why people want to read all this stuff about weddings and junk.'

'I *like* weddings,' Candy said. 'The bride always—' She stopped suddenly and stared at the paragraph she had almost passed over. 'Art Institute to purchase new paintings' read the small heading. The paper was dated May 5.

The others, who had looked up when she stopped talking, scrambled over to see what she was reading:

> The Modern Art Institute, home of the greatest collection of modern paintings in the state, will shortly conclude the purchase of three new paintings, it was announced today by Mr. Guy Howard, Curator of the Institute.
>
> A fourth painting has already been acquired, Mr. Howard said, but it will not be publicly shown until Sunday, June 20, when it will be displayed with the other three at the Modern Art Institute. Mr. Howard did not reveal the precise amount paid for this one painting, but indicated that it was in the neighborhood of $10,000.
>
> The Modern Art Institute was established in 1901 by Mr. John A. Howard, father of the present curator. In 1925, thanks to a growing pride in Capitol City as an art centre, a Society of Friends of Art was formed. Contributions are made each year to the Institute for the buying of new pictures. Upon Mr. John Howard's death in 1926, his son Guy became Curator of the Institute. Extensive study in the United States and Europe has made Mr. Guy Howard an outstanding connoisseur of modern painting.

'Gee whillikers!' exclaimed Huggy, who had skipped the last paragraph. 'Ten thousand buckeroos for one little ole painting. And to think of Uncle Guy getting his sticky paws on that money!'

'Sunday, June twentieth,' said Ellen. 'And Uncle Guy said Uncle Martin had to finish his painting by Friday night —why, that's tomorrow! We've got to get *busy*.'

'Look, it's almost stopped raining!' Candy ran over to the window to look out. While they had been going through the newspapers, the rain had slackened and the sky begun to clear. As they watched, the light grew brighter and brighter.

'What are we waiting for?' asked John. 'Let's get a move on.'

But before they had got into boots and raincoats, Mrs. Norland appeared, arms akimbo. 'Them as gits papers out better put 'em back, quicklike. Pick up after you I won't, and that's flat. Skit now and put them back in the cellarway the way you found them. And I don't wanta see them falling down the steps, neither.'

By the time they had restored the papers to a neat bundle on the shelf in the cellarway, another shower came up, but it didn't last long, and finally they were on their way to the tunnel. Addle joined them joyfully as soon as they emerged from the kitchen door, smearing them with muddy paw-prints.

The rain started again while they were still in the woods, and the gloom of the trees became denser than ever. Ellen, always practical, thought they should turn back, and John looked dubious, but Candy joined with Huggy to insist that they go on. Even if they couldn't get to Howard Hall, she had an idea she wanted to try out. By the time they got to the clearing, they had to run full tilt to the shelter of the log cabin.

'Now what?' asked Ellen when they were crowded wetly inside. The rain thumped noisily on the roof and sprayed at them through one of the windows.

Candy picked up the trowel from the stack of tools they had left in the corner. 'I've got sort of an idea,' she said mysteriously, as she struggled out of her wet raincoat, switching the trowel from hand to hand.

They stared at her in amazement.

'Hey, remember? We already dug out the tunnel,' Huggy said.

Candy sat down on the edge of the opening, and let herself slide down into the tunnel.

John looked at her thoughtfully. 'Mind if we come along?' He reached for the spade.

'Yeah,' Huggy chimed in. 'You'll get lonely with just an idea to keep you comp'ny.'

'Besides, you'll need some light.' Ellen took a stubby candle and a box of matches off the shelf. 'Okay?'

'All right,' Candy said, though she rather wished they wouldn't come along, in case her idea didn't work out. They might make fun of her. She felt her way cautiously along the tunnel. It was pitch dark except for the dim light that filtered in at the other end. It was scary down here, and she was glad the others were following her. In a moment she heard the scratch of a match as Ellen lit the candle. Their shadows leaped ahead and crawled grotesquely on the walls.

At the middle of the tunnel, where it narrowed, Candy dropped to her knees. She measured with her eye to find the exact centre between the walls, and dug the trowel into the ground. The blade went in only about an inch and chipped out a hard piece of earth.

'Shoulda brought some dynamite,' Huggy said. 'What're you digging for, anyway? Uranium?'

'Here.' John pushed forward with the spade he had caught up before sliding into the tunnel after the others. 'Want me to try with this?'

'Yes.' Candy stepped back. 'Please,' she added.

The ground was solidly packed from their footsteps and the treads of those other four so long ago. John chopped at it with the point of the spade, and little chips of dirt flew out. Ellen put the candle on the floor, and Huggy slumped down against the wall with a great sigh.

'Real comfy it is down here, too,' he said. 'Course, after about six weeks, when you've dug out a coupla inches, we might go back to Summer House, just for a visit, y'unnerstand—I really *like* it here, it's so cosy.' The others made no answer, and there was only the chop-chop of the spade and John's heavy breathing to be heard. After a long while, Huggy ran his hand over his chin. 'Yep, just as I thought. Whiskers. You guys ever hear of Rip Van Winkle?'

'Hush,' said Ellen. 'It's raining too hard to go out anyway. Why don't you take a turn with the spade?'

'What? Little ole me dig just for the sake of digging? Why doesn't somebody say what we're looking *for*?'

John paused and wiped his face with his arm. 'Why don't you figure it out for yourself like the rest of us?'

Huggy sat up straight. 'You mean *you* know? Hey, what is this? Do you know, too, Ellen?'

She nodded. 'I think so.'

Huggy sat back, disgruntled, and John went on picking at the earth. He finally got the spade deeper into the ground by standing on it. Huggy gave a weak cheer and went back to thinking and muttering to himself. 'Maybe we're trying to get to China,' he murmured. 'Or digging a well in case we get thirsty. A little ole well full of coca-cola would be nice . . .'

Candy and Ellen suddenly leaned forward over the hole John had dug. Metal gleamed where John had knicked it with the spade.

'It's a box!' Ellen cried. 'A tin box! Oh, Candy, you clever thing to think of its being here!'

Huggy scrambled over to the hole to look. 'My golly, you mean there really *is* something? What is it? Treasure?'

'Sort of,' said John. 'Here, you dig awhile, and you can have one-fourth of what's inside.'

Huggy took the spade eagerly and began jabbing at the hard-packed dirt. 'Ohboyohboyohboyohboy. Hidden treasure. This is terrific!' He stood with both feet on the spade until it sank into the ground, and then jumped up and down on it. In the flickering light from the candle, and with his short hair on end and his glasses crooked over his bright blue eyes, he looked like a gleeful gnome. Suddenly the ground gave beneath him, and he went flying backwards with the spade clutched in his hands. While he disentangled himself the others peered anxiously into the hole.

'It's all right,' John said. 'You didn't break the box, and look, it's all uncovered now. We've just got to dig around the sides.'

Huggy got stiffly to his feet. 'Please don't worry about poor ole Pindar, will you? I only busted my back in three places, but don't let that spoil your pleasure . . .' He stared at the metal box embedded in the earth. It was only about five inches square. 'Pretty small treasure. I . . . Hey!' He snatched the trowel from Candy's hand and began to prod around the box. 'I just caught on,' he said breathlessly. 'My gosh, I f'got all about what the diary said. But how did you figure out exactly where to dig?'

'Well,' said Candy, 'I just thought of where *we* would bury something like that, and the very middle of the tunnel seemed like a good idea.'

John had his scout knife out and was probing all around the box with it, while Huggy pried with the trowel. A moment more and the box moved slightly. Huggy slipped the trowel in deeper and lifted.

'It's coming,' Ellen said. 'Be careful you don't break it.'

Two more tugs, and the box was out. Ellen brought the candle near so that they could examine it better. It was black with age and encrusted with dirt. There was some kind of rotted cloth clinging to it, as though it had once been wrapped up. There was no lock, but the lid was stuck fast, glued to the box by dirt and damp during the long years underground. John solemnly handed his scout knife to Candy to do the honours of prying the box open. It took some minutes to force the lid, but it finally gave with a grating sound that set their teeth on edge. Inside were four small bundles of oilskin, stiff with age now, but still protecting their contents. Candy hesitated and then handed one of the bundles to each of the other children to open. With fingers that trembled with excitement, she carefully began to unroll her own bundle.

When at last she had removed the last fold of oilskin, she stared, bewildered, at the small dark object which fell into her hand. It was a carved piece of wood about three inches long.

'Gee-money,' said Huggy, 'but what is it?' He was staring at his prize. It was shaped much like Candy's, but what it was other than a flat carved head of a man with a hole through it for an eye, none of them knew.

Ellen's and John's packages gave up two more carved heads. Silently they laid them out beside Candy's and Huggy's and stared at them.

'That's queer,' said John slowly. 'Seems to me I've seen one of these before, but I can't remember—I believe they're some sort of good-luck charm.'

'But the diary said W-W's,' Candy pointed out. 'So they must have a real name.'

'They look such awfully *worried* little men,' said Ellen. 'I thought good-luck pieces would be cheerful smiling things.'

'They're worried, all right.' Huggy picked his up. It was made of mahogany, and polished smooth, but it was obviously hand-carved.

'Worried,' Candy repeated. 'Maybe that's one of the W's! Worried-Women. Worried-Witches, Worried—'

'Wombats,' Huggy suggested. 'Or Wallabys, or—'

'Worts! Worried-*Worts*!' John said triumphantly. 'I mean *Worry*-Worts.'

'Huh?' Huggy stared at him. 'What's a wart got to be worried about?'

'Not that kind,' said John. 'And I remember where I saw one—it's in a box Mom has, full of old letters and pictures and things. I think my Dad gave it to her.'

'Yes, but what *is* it?' insisted Huggy.

'Well, people who worry all the time are called worry-worts, so—'

'So if you make a special Worry-Wort,' Ellen interrupted, 'it will be something like a good-luck piece because it'll do all your worrying for you!'

They sat looking at the four heads with pleased smiles. Then Huggy picked his up and rubbed it lovingly with his thumb. 'Ohboyohboyohboy, I sure can use you at school. You can worry and worry and worry, and ole Pindar will take life easy.'

'Until you get your grades,' Ellen said. She put her little man in her pocket and patted it. 'It's really comforting to have a Worry-Wort, isn't it? I'm going to carry mine *for ever*.' She jumped to her feet. 'I wonder if it's still pouring outside.' She stepped over Huggy's and John's legs and walked towards the Howard opening of the tunnel. 'It's still raining *very* hard,' she called back from the end. 'But you did a good job on the log pile. Hardly any rain comes in the opening. I don't think there's much sense in going to

Howard—' She suddenly stopped talking with a little squeak of surprise.

'What's the matter?' John called in a loud whisper.

Ellen was on her knees, examining something that lay on the floor of the tunnel. 'It's a message,' she said, 'tied around a rock and thrown into the tunnel. Bring the light, quick!'

John snatched up the candle and they stumbled over each other to reach her. With careful fingers, Ellen was removing the twine that tied the paper to the small rock. In a moment it was free. Ellen turned the paper over and spread it out flat, smoothing out the wrinkles.

'It's from Heather,' said Candy, pointing to the signature at the bottom. 'Hurry up and read it.'

Ellen read:

> 'Aunt Ruth is hiding her head in a feather bed because of the storm, so I'm going to nip out while I have a chance and leave this note for you in your tunnel. She is taking me to Capitol City to shop and go to a cinema, so I won't be able to see you today. They are watching me very closely and I think something *queer* is going on. It's something to do with Uncle Martin's studio and he is afraid of Uncle Guy. Aunt Ruth says she is taking me away somewhere on Saturday for a holiday and I don't want to go. I must fly before the lightning stops and Aunt Ruth crawls out of her feather bed to look for me.
>
> 'Heaps of love,
> 'Heather Lyne-Howard.'

12

FRENCHY AND LIB

'LOOK AT the rain,' Huggy said. They were back in the drawing-room of Summer House, drinking hot chocolate before the big fire John had built. Shortly after they found Heather's note, there had been a lull in the rain and they made a dash for home, but the rain swept down upon them again as they left the woods and soaked them in spite of their raincoats and boots. Mrs. Norland was cross over the puddles they made on her clean kitchen floor, until Candy sneezed, and then she bundled them all upstairs and into hot baths.

Now they were warm and dry and sleepy, but John said they should get to work on the rest of Low's diary. The others grumbled because they wanted to talk over their adventures, and Huggy called John a slave-driver, but he was adamant.

So in a few moments they were gathered around the big coffee table once more, copying out the code on to fresh sheets of paper so that each of them could be working on a different part of the diary.

Then there was silence except for the crackle of the fire, the drum of rain on the windows, the whisper of pencil on paper, and several prodigious yawns from Huggy. After a long time, John announced, 'I've got something. It seems to be the next summer after they built the tunnel. July twenty-seventh. Listen:

> 'We were playing underground railway and Guy was a Southern planter while the rest of us were escaping slaves. He kept kicking us and twisting our arms and then he pushed Lib into the tunnel and she hit her head on the edge of the trapdoor and it knocked her out. Guy wouldn't let us run for help, but I got away and ran all the way to Howard Hall. Mr. Howard came back with me and carried Lib home, but she's all right, just a big bump on her head. We didn't dare tell him it was Guy's fault for fear of what Guy would do to us, so we all got lectured on playing too rough, and afterwards Guy tripped me into the tunnel for giving away the secret of the underground railway. Mr. Howard said he would block up the tunnel if there were any more accidents.'

'Too bad he didn't,' Huggy said. 'You can just see old Guy working up to that cave-in.'

Ellen made a funny little half-smothered sound, and then

I

bent over the page she was working on, her pencil scribbling furiously.

'What've you got?' asked Candy, but Ellen shook her head and went on with her scrawl. She was working straight from the diary now, decoding the last few pages of the book.

John and Huggy started to gather up the papers they had all worked on, putting them in order by date. Candy watched for a while and then wandered over to the bookshelves and began pulling books out at random, leafing through them, reading a few lines, and then returning them to their places. There were lots of old-fashioned books on the lowest shelf, peopled with ink-drawn children in odd-looking clothes. Candy got interested in a gold-leaved volume of *The Water Babies* and sat down cross-legged before the shelves to turn over the thick pages. Faintly, overhead, came the whine of Mrs. Norland's vacuum cleaner, while rain still tapped at the windows.

'Finished!' Ellen announced at last, flexing her tired fingers. 'Wait till you hear this part!' She began to read. Huggy and John sat back expectantly; Candy, by the bookshelves, idly turned the pages of her book as she listened.

'It is two days after Christmas, nineteen hundred and seventeen. The holiday is going very fast. The Howards gave a big party on Christmas Eve, but Guy said it was baby stuff for him and went around bossing everybody. He keeps showing off about shaving, especially in front of the new French girl the Howards have sort of adopted. She's a 42nd cousin or something and always lived in France till her mother died last summer and now she is going to live at Howard Hall. She is only eight but very smart and she will do anything Martin tells her. She says she is going to marry him and keep his paint brushes clean. We started to tease her about it, but Martin got very fierce and said he would knock us down if we didn't let her alone.'

'Doesn't he say what her name is?' John asked in a queer voice.

Ellen shook her head. 'Not yet. Wait till I read more. This next part is in 1918:

> 'The fifteenth of June. Martin won honorable mention in the Five-States Painting Exhibition. He is the youngest painter ever to win that, only fifteen. He says he couldn't have done it if it wasn't for Frenchy. Guy said that was a good joke because the picture was a portrait of Frenchy, but Lib and I knew what Martin meant. Guy keeps trying to butt in between Mart and Frenchy. He doesn't like it because Martin sometimes stands up to him now. Guy swiped Frenchy's old doll and buried it, and Martin begged him to give it back but he wouldn't and then Frenchy hit Guy on the head with her fist and Guy twisted her arm and Martin socked him right in the nose. First time Mart ever got in a fight. We all cheered for him.'

Ellen paused to pick up another sheet of paper. 'This part is a whole year later, in September 1919.

> 'Lib is going away to finishing school next week, and Guy is sailing for Europe the week after to study for a year. He is going to take over the Modern Art Institute eventually and has to study for several years all about painting. Martin's painting master wants him to go to Europe to study, but Guy said he wasn't going to be a wet-nurse for a sixteen-year-old punk painter, so Martin can't go. He doesn't seem to mind. He's bound to be a great painter and marry Frenchy and live in Paris. I enter the University of Virginia this fall.'

Candy heard this part with only half an ear, for she was staring at the inscription in the front of *The Water Babies*. With a thoughtful frown she pulled several other old books off the shelf and opened the covers.

Ellen was reading on:

> 'July thirtieth, nineteen hundred and twenty. I have just found this old journal in Underground Station 2 and thought it would be amusing to make another entry if I can remember how to do the code. Today is my eighteenth birthday. Mother and Dad gave me a watch and chain. I have a date with Lib in half an hour, but we are going to meet in her garden because of Guy, who has taken a great dislike to me since he got back from Europe last month. This is because he was making fun of Martin's small-time dabbling, as he called it, and I lost my temper. I told him he was a pompous, conceited, bullying, second-rate liar, and if Martin didn't turn out to be a great painter it would be his fault. This is something I've wanted to tell him for years, but I never had the words for it before. Guy didn't dare start a scrap because I'm bigger than he is now, and stronger. But he warned me to stay away from Howard Hall. I wouldn't be surprised to find the tunnel blocked up one of these nights when I'm on my way to meet Lib.'

'The cave-in!' Huggy exclaimed. 'That's how Guy was going to block up the tunnel. Just to get even with Low. What'll you bet he took off those braces right then and went off somewhere so nobody could blame him when the ceiling fell in!'

Ellen nodded. 'You're probably right. This next part is the very last entry in the whole diary:

> 'August second. Guy left yesterday for a trip around the country visiting art museums. Everybody breathed a big sigh

of relief, especially Martin, who is so used to being bossed that he can't stop knuckling under, unless it's something to do with Frenchy. I don't like the way Guy looks at little Frenchy. He will do all he can to separate her from Martin. But I promised Frenchy not to call her that any more, now that she is much more grown up and is going away to school soon. She insists on being Jacqueline.'

Ellen's voice stopped and there was a startled silence. Then—

'My mother came to America when she was little,' John said quietly, 'and she went to live with some relatives, but she never talks about them. I've never even heard their names. But *her* name is Jacqueline!'

'Garsh!' Huggy exclaimed, his blue eyes bright with excitement. 'Why, Uncle Martin Howard might have been your father if— Gee-money, John, this makes you sort of pratic'ly a part of the mystery. Hey, listen, I've got an idea! You know what Uncle Guy said about their next-door neighbour just waiting for a chance to even things up? Well, he musta meant your Mom! I'll bet that's the reason she keeps on coming here every summer. Maybe she's going to get Uncle Martin away from Uncle Guy after all! Sure, that must be it!'

'No, it's not,' Candy said. Her arms full of books, she walked purposefully towards them, let the books fall in a heap on the table. 'Uncle Guy meant Mrs. Summer, all right. Look at what I discovered.' She flipped open the covers of the books, one after the other.

They were all inscribed in childish handwriting:

Lib Howard.

But the last volume Candy opened, a volume of Saki's short stories, read:

To my dear wife Lib from Lowell, 1921.

13

'JOLLY EXCITING'

FRIDAY MORNING was dull grey, but the rain had stopped. After breakfast, the children rushed through the dishes and the few chores that Mrs. Addams found for them.

Mrs. Summer came into the kitchen just as they were finishing the last of their tasks. Candy's heart sank and she quickly rubbed her thumb and finger over the Worry-Wort in her pocket, because Mrs. Summer looked the way Mrs. Bascombe did when she was about to say Candy couldn't do something she especially wanted to. But Mrs. S.'s first words were encouraging.

'You all look healthy enough after your soaking yesterday.'

'Yep,' John said promptly. 'We should have our heads
examined for getting caught like that. We won't do it again,
thanks.'

'Good.' Mrs. Summer smiled. 'I know what fun it can be
playing in the woods, so I'm not going to put down any
restrictions except that you be sensible. I think I can depend
on you, can't I?'

'Yes,' they chorused.

'Very well. We have some final matters to settle today in
the city. When we finish . . .' She paused and then shook
her head. 'No, I'll tell you tomorrow. Be sure to wear your
raincoats if you go out. Mrs. Norland will be here for the
day to look after you.'

Released at last, they set off for the woods. Addle joined
them, leaping and barking joyously. Ellen stopped short.

'What about Addle? Won't he give us away if we take
him?'

'Of course he won't,' Huggy said indignantly. 'Poor
Addle. If he stays home, so do I.' He knelt to hug Addle,
but the dog gave his cheek a swipe with his long pink
tongue and scampered away to tear around in circles.

'He'll soon wear himself out and be quiet,' Huggy said.
'I'll speak to him before we go through the tunnel.'

When they reached the log cabin, it started to rain again,
but gently.

'That's all right,' Ellen said. 'The rain will keep Uncle
Guy out of the woods. And the trees are so thick we won't
get very wet. It isn't like yesterday's rain. I wish we'd worn
our rubbers, though.'

Huggy got hold of Addle, who had frisked himself out
for the moment, and whispered confidentially in his ear.

This was difficult because Addle kept trying to lick Huggy's nose. At last Huggy rose, hitched his belt, and pushed up his glasses.

'He understands now,' Huggy announced. 'He promised to stick close to us and not to bark.'

One by one they slid into the hole with Addle coming last. They groped their way cautiously to the other end, where John stuck his head out carefully and listened. There was no sound except for the soft splat of rain on the logs.

A minute later they were all standing in the shelter of an oak on the Howard estate. John had his compass in hand.

'As far as I can make out, Howard Hall is due east. The tunnel seems to be on a straight line between the houses. Better notice any landmarks like different-looking trees. Everybody ready?'

They nodded solemnly. Addle stood up and waggled his stubby tail. John started off, the rest following in single file. Candy tried to pretend she was really on the nice safe Summer side of the wall. These were just ordinary trees, exactly like those in the Summer woods, she told herself, fingering the comforting curves of her Worry-Wort.

Only they weren't. They were unfriendly monstrous trees, waiting in the gloomy woods to close in on the children and swallow them up. Addle pushed his cold wet nose into her hand and looked up at her anxiously.

'It's all right, Addle,' she whispered, giving him a reassuring pat. Addle's damp doggy smell made her feel better.

They walked unendingly, it seemed to Candy. Sometimes they had to detour from the compass direction because of fallen trees and then John would pause to figure out how many degrees they had gone off course before leading them back. Candy tried to memorize trees, like the two sycamore sentinels on either side of a dead elm, but most of them looked alike. She tried scuffing up the old leaves to make a trail, but that made so much noise that she stopped. They should have brought pebbles, like Hansel and Gretel, to strew along the path.

Ellen, who was walking in front of her, stopped short, and Candy banged into her.

'Sh-h,' said Ellen and pointed to the left, where the trees thinned out.

Looming up in the grey mistiness of the rain were the stone walls of an immense house. The windows were pinched narrow eyes, set in recesses. The walls went up and up like the walls of a gloomy old castle, and on each corner was a round stone turret. They had reached Howard Hall!

John looked all around as though memorizing their position and then motioned the others forward. Slowly, and keeping well back within the fringe of trees, they started to circle the house. Their first sight of it had been from the rear. As they rounded it, they saw that the gravelled drive which circled the house made a loop directly in front of it and then led off in the direction of the gate and road. The grass in the centre of the loop was long and unkempt.

John stopped suddenly, and they almost piled up on each other again. Addle whined softly and crept closer to Huggy.

There was a pale-green station wagon drawn up by the front steps. As they watched from the shield of trees, the big door of the house swung slowly open and a man stepped out. He stood for a moment on the box of a porch, as though examining the weather. He was tall and thin, with a narrow head. He wore no hat, and his black hair curled crisply. After a moment he jerked up the collar of his mackintosh and dashed down the steps to the car. There was the whirr of the starter, the zoom of a powerful motor, and the station wagon rolled off. They watched it out of sight down the gravelled drive.

'Uncle Guy?' John queried softly.

Ellen nodded. 'Must be. He looks just like his voice.'

They watched a few minutes longer, but nothing else happened, so they walked on until they came to the outer drive. They didn't want to cross the drive in full view of anyone who might be watching, so they retraced their steps to circle the house in the opposite direction. On the other side of Howard Hall they passed along the back of a long low grey stone building set beside the drive—a garage, they decided from the wheel tracks on the gravel. The old stone walls of the house showed no signs of life. The children stood and stared at the blank front through the veiling mist.

'What should we do now?' Huggy whispered.

Candy was looking up at the third floor windows. 'Is this the north side of the house?' she asked.

John consulted his compass. 'Yes. Why?'

'See that big window up there?' She pointed. 'It's the only really big window in the whole house, and it gets the north light, so it must be where Uncle Martin does all his painting. My art teacher says a north light is best, so—'

'By jingo,' breathed Huggy, 'little old Needle-nose is right. So if that's the art department, that's where Uncle Martin will be and we'll know how to keep out of his sight.'

'But that leaves Aunt Ruth, doesn't it?' Ellen asked.

As though in answer to her question, the big front door opened again and a tall blonde woman emerged, carrying a pencil-slim umbrella and a huge handbag. She looked terribly dressed-up, Candy thought—what her mother called 'arty', and her face had a drawn look, as though she didn't eat enough and stayed up too late and smoked too many cigarettes. Just like Candy's Aunt Janet, even to the earrings they could see from where they stood. The woman stood on the top step, reflectively drawing on her gloves. Then she tripped down the steps in her high heels and walked around on the drive to the long grey stone building.

There were sounds of a car starting, and a yellow convertible appeared, sleek and glossy. It rolled down the gravelled drive and out of sight.

'Auntie Ruth,' Candy and John announced together.

'Wonder if there's anybody else, like a housekeeper,' Ellen said.

'We'll have to take a chance,' said John. 'Let's circle the house again.'

They saw no more than they had the last time, but at least the rain had stopped.

'For goodness' sake,' Ellen said, 'if we're going to see Heather, we'll have to do *something*. That woman might come back any minute, or Uncle Guy. Why don't we try walking around on the grass, except for the front of the house where Uncle Martin is.'

'What if he's not *in* his studio?' asked Huggy.

'That's a thought,' said John. 'But then he's really on Heather's side, so— Come on. As soon as we're out of sight of that big window, we'll walk right around on the grass.'

Candy tried to shrink herself up to half her size when she moved out of the woods behind Ellen. It was terrifying, walking out in the open, not knowing who was behind those squeezed-in windows looking out at them. They walked right around the sides and back of the house again, staring at all the windows. Addle tagged obediently at their heels, as though he knew that this was serious business. Then they stopped uncertainly at the left front corner. Candy could feel her feet squelching in her shoes.

'Maybe one of us should try to get inside,' John said dubiously.

'If we just knew where Heather's room was—' Ellen looked nervously over her shoulder at the empty stone garage. 'I don't like this.'

'You know,' said Candy, 'I can see Howard Hall from my—I mean our—window at home, and the day I—I mean we—talked to Heather, she said something about us living in "that big house", so maybe she saw it from her room the same way I keep looking at this place. I mean—'

'I get it,' Huggy interrupted. 'Maybe her room's on this side of the house.'

John looked up the towering height of the massive stone wall. 'She'd have to be way up on the third floor to see Summer House because it's not as high as this one. Well, heck, it's worth a try.' He picked up a handful of gravel and walked back along the side of the house until he stood halfway between front and back. 'Here goes nothing,' he said and let fly with a piece of gravel. It landed with a chink squarely against the middle window of the third storey.

Nothing happened.

John moved to another window and tried again. Still nothing. Huggy tossed a few stones, but they fell short of the mark. Back and forth they moved, from window to window, while John threw stone after stone.

'It's making an awful racket,' Ellen whispered. 'Maybe we ought to try the back of the house.'

'Wait!' John said suddenly. 'Look up there.' He was pointing to the top windows of the round stone turret that formed the back corner of the house. Behind one of them was a figure making signs at them. It had to be Heather Lyne-Howard!

John made window-opening motions, but the girl shrugged and pointed.

'She wants us to go around back,' Ellen said. They ran around the turret and stood looking up. One of the windows at the top opened slowly outward, and Heather's head appeared. She had softly waving fair hair that swung about her face as she leaned over.

'*Hel*lo,' she called down to them. 'I'm locked in.'

'What's happened?' John asked as softly as he could, cupping his hands around his mouth to direct his voice towards her.

'Uncle Guy was furious because I disobeyed and went out of the window.' She laughed. 'He doesn't know about yesterday, though. Did you get my note?'

'Yes. We think you're very brave. Is Uncle Martin at home?'

'I suppose so. He never goes out. I say, there's something terribly queer going on.'

'I know. Can we get in?'

She thought about it. 'Better not. Auntie Ruth's just gone down the road to shop. She's coming right back.'

The children looked anxiously around, but no sound broke the silence.

'What is Uncle Martin painting?' asked Candy.

Heather shrugged. 'I can't find out.'

'Well, listen,' John said, 'we think you might be in danger.'

'Really? It sounds jolly exciting!' She leaned farther out of the window. 'What sort of danger?'

'We're not sure. But you ought to be careful and play dumb.' John looked askance at Addle, who had risen to his feet and seemed to be listening intently to some sound the rest couldn't hear. 'We've got to go. Can you get out any time at all?'

'I'll try. Maybe this afternoon. I'll tell Auntie Ruth I get ill without lots of fresh air. But she won't let me go far.'

'We'll be back at two o'clock,' John said hastily. Now they could hear the faint whine of an automobile in the distance. 'In the woods—right there.' He pointed. 'And see if you can get a look at what Uncle Martin is doing. Only be careful of Uncle Guy.'

'Very well, I'll do my best. What is your dog's name?'

'Addle.'

Heather laughed. 'Good-bye, then. Good-bye, Addle!' She blew a kiss at them.

They could hear the bite of tyres on gravel now, and scampered across the wet grass to the safety of the trees. Addle turned to look back, but they frantically whistled to him and he came, reluctantly.

From the screen of trees, they saw the yellow convertible swing around the corner and stop almost where they had been standing. The arty Aunt Ruth stepped out, one hand fumbling in her large bag. She shook it with annoyance, peering inside. As if to plague her further, the rain began to patter down again. With a gesture of impatience, Aunt Ruth hurried over to the shelter of the overhang that roofed a sort of stone-flagged terrace in front of the door. Reaching up, she felt around one of the timbers. Withdrawing her hand, she went to the door and unlocked it.

'Now put it back,' John breathed. 'Be a sport and put the key back, Aunt Ruth.'

But instead, Aunt Ruth scurried back to the car to fetch two big bags, one of which sprouted celery tops. They watched her go into the house and kick the door shut with one foot. The key was still in the lock. They waited for long minutes, but Aunt Ruth didn't reappear.

Addle began to get restless, but Huggy lifted one floppy

ear and whispered at length. Addle lay down again with a hang-dog expression and sighed heavily.

'I've got to have that key,' John said suddenly. 'This may be our only chance to snag it.'

Ellen was horrified. 'Oh no! She'll see you and besides, even if she didn't, she'd miss the key and know it was stolen.'

'No, she wouldn't,' Candy spoke up. 'My Aunt Janet is always losing her keys, and she's just like that Aunt Ruth—you know, arty, sort of. She'll just think she took it inside and put it down somewhere. Look, you can tell how careless she is—she left the car window open.'

'Hold Addle,' John said. 'I'm going to try for it.'

'Shaddap,' said Huggy. 'Here she comes again.'

The door had opened. Aunt Ruth hurried out to the car, hastily rolled up the window and rushed back to shelter again. At the door she noticed the key, extracted it from the lock, and went on in.

'Fathead,' Huggy muttered. 'Whoops, wait a minute.'

The door opened once more. Aunt Ruth had reconsidered. She stepped out and reached up to the rafter nearest to her. This time when she went in, she closed the door with a final bang.

'Whoosh!' said Huggy. 'I almost rubbed the nose off my Worry-Wort. Let's get out of here. All this excitement's made me so hungry my backbone's clattering around in front of my stomick.'

They set off with John and his compass in the lead. After five minutes of silent plodding in their squelchy shoes, they decided that they were far enough away from Howard Hall to talk.

'She didn't take it very seriously—about the danger, did she?' said Ellen.

'Jolly exciting, she called it,' Huggy grumbled. 'I wish

she would put on my shoes for about five minutes. Jolly wet, if you ask me.'

'Do you really think she is in danger, John?' Candy asked.

John paused, looked back at them. 'You heard Uncle Guy talking to Uncle Martin, didn't you? And you read the diary and you know about the cave-in on Low. Well, what do *you* think?'

Candy shivered. They didn't talk any more.

14

LOST . . .

At two o'clock they were waiting in the woods behind Howard Hall for Heather to appear.

At two-thirty they were still waiting. Huggy declared that he had rubbed his Worry-Wort so hard there was nothing left but the hole in it. They had chosen a spot from which they could see the back door and Heather's open window in the turret. Once they thought they saw her, but they couldn't be sure. It was damp and cool amidst the trees, and they shivered in their mackintoshes. Addle, his head on his paws, watched them anxiously, cocking his eyebrows from one to another.

When Heather finally came into sight, she came from around the house and—Aunt Ruth was with her! The children stifled a groan and flattened themselves.

'Won't you play quoits with me, Auntie Ruth?' Heather's clear voice carried to them. 'It's ever so much fun, really!'

'My dear child,' came Aunt Ruth's husky voice, 'I can scarcely play games in these heels.'

'Then do change your shoes, oh do, please, Auntie Ruth. You'll adore it, if you just play once.' She tossed a bright yellow rubber quoit into the air and raced across the grass to catch it.

'It's much too wet,' Aunt Ruth said. 'But I'll stand here and watch you.'

'Oh dear, I *wish* I had somebody to play with. Aren't there any children around here that we could invite for tea? What about that house next door?'

'I've told you before, there's nobody but a mad old woman over there.'

'Well, couldn't I go and call on her? I know heaps of mad old women in England. They always have the loveliest tarts and scones and things, and almost always a parrot.'

'No, you can't,' Aunt Ruth said shortly. 'She's dangerous.'

'America isn't much fun, is it?' Heather said sadly.

'It will be when we go to the mountains tomorrow, and your Uncle Guy will come too as soon as—' She stopped short, and then went on: 'You can have long hikes and cook over an open fire and—'

'No other children?'

'I'm afraid we don't know any children your age. I'm sorry, Heather.'

'Let's take a walk in the woods, Auntie Ruth. The trees smell perfectly heavenly when they're wet.'

'*Not* in these shoes.'

'Then let me,' Heather begged. 'Just the *teeniest* little walk.'

'No.' Aunt Ruth sounded nervous. 'Your Uncle Guy is afraid for you to walk in the woods. Because of the rattle-snakes.'

'But how can there be rattlesnakes? The book I read last night said that all the rattlesnakes are in Texas and places like that.'

'Well, copperheads then. You can *not* go, and that's final. Play with your quoit like a good girl. We'll have to go in soon. It's damp.'

The children had their eyes glued on Heather. She looked to be about ten years old, though she sounded much older, probably because of her quick crisp way of talking. She was slim and sturdy in her grey pleated skirt and blue jacket, which had some sort of emblem worked on the breast pocket. There was a beret on her head, but it didn't hide her taffy-coloured hair which curled under at her shoulders. She had an impish little face and sparky blue eyes.

Each time, as she threw the quoit into the air, she moved closer to the trees and the children. Addle stood up in quivering excitement, eager to join the game, but Huggy wrapped an arm about him and talked soothingly in whispers.

When Heather got quite close to the trees, she shrilled, 'Watch this one, Auntie Ruth,' and threw the quoit wildly into the air. It fell down through the branches and caught, swaying on a limb.

'Oh, beastly luck!' Heather cried. 'It's in the tree, Auntie Ruth! I know, I'll find a branch to poke it loose.' Before Aunt Ruth could answer, she had run into the woods, straight towards the children. They gasped at her daring. What if Aunt Ruth came running after her! But Heather

seemed to know the full extent of Aunt Ruth's love for her
high heels. She only stood on the gravelled drive and called
to Heather to come back and let Uncle Martin retrieve the
quoit for her. Heather paid no attention, but cast about for
a suitable dead branch. Her search led directly to the children, but she didn't look at them.

'I can't get rid of her—horrid thing!' she said out of the
side of her mouth. Her blue eyes snapped with anger.

'Did you get into your uncle's studio?' John whispered.

'No. He even had lunch there. I think he's locked in, too.'
She raised her voice to shout at Aunt Ruth. 'I won't be a
minute. Here's a branch—no, it's too short.' She threw down
the stick she had picked up and looked farther.

'But whatever he's been doing, it must be finished,' she
whispered. 'Because I heard Uncle Guy telling him to "keep
his hands off it so it would dry" this morning after breakfast.
And when I came down to lunch with Aunt Ruth, I could
hear Uncle Martin just walking back and forth in the studio.
I asked what sort of picture he was painting, but Auntie
Ruth said he was very touchy about his paintings and never
let anybody see them.'

'Heather!' called Aunt Ruth. 'You must come back—
instantly!'

'Very well, Auntie Ruth,' Heather said cheerfully. 'I
think I've found a good branch now. You ought to come
here—there's a lovely greeny dampy smell.' She stood up
straight and breathed deeply for Aunt Ruth's benefit.

'Listen,' John whispered hurriedly. 'Could you sneak out
tonight after dark?'

'Perhaps,' but she sounded dubious. 'If I'm not locked in.'
She picked up a long branch and started skinning off the
shoots.

'Heather!' cried Aunt Ruth.

'Coming,' Heather sang out, and stripped a few more shoots from her branch.

'If you can't get out,' John said hastily, 'we'll try to get in. We're going to take you to Summer House with us. About ten-thirty.'

Heather's blue eyes widened, but all she said was, 'Very well. I'll be ready,' and dragging her branch, walked back towards the tree that held her quoit.

The children watched her fish for it until Aunt Ruth's patience gave out, and then the quoit came tumbling down. She could have got it easily on the first try if she had wanted, they knew, but she deliberately swung at the wrong limbs to annoy Aunt Ruth. They all nodded approvingly. Aunt Ruth would be fun to annoy.

But that was the end of seeing Heather for the afternoon. Aunt Ruth took her off around the house on the plea that it was much too damp to stay outside longer.

The rest of the day dragged along as though time had got stuck. The sun, after sulking all day, decided to show itself about three-thirty, and then made up for its bad behaviour by shining so hotly that the children changed into shorts and T-shirts. As the afternoon wore on, Candy felt more and more excited. She had never dreamed there could be such an adventure in real life.

Mrs. Summer and Mrs. Addams returned from Capitol City and Mrs. Norland left after reporting that her four charges had been exemplary children except that they seemed to think they were ducks instead of human beings.

At last it was dinner-time, and the children began to carry out their plan for getting out of the house. They made a great show of sleepiness which Huggy almost overdid by pretending to fall asleep over his dessert.

'Gracious,' said Mrs. Summer, 'don't let your head drop

into your pudding. What did you find to do in the woods on such a wet day?'

'We're making trails,' Ellen said truthfully. They certainly *had* been making trails.

'Then we thought we'd draw a map,' Huggy embroidered the story. 'See, like this . . .' He dug a stub of pencil out of his pocket and pushed his dish aside to draw on the tablecloth.

'Never mind,' said Mrs. Summer hastily. 'You can show me better on paper some other time.'

With an innocent look of disappointment, Huggy moved his dish back and gave Candy a fierce wink across the table.

John gave a stupendous yawn as they got up from the table. 'Whew! Am I tired!'

'Me too,' said Candy. 'I could go to sleep standing on my head.' She stretched her arms and fetched up the largest yawn she was capable of.

Mrs. Summer glanced around at the four of them with a half-suppressed smile. 'If this extraordinary show of sleepiness means that you're planning a raid on the refrigerator tonight, better stay away from the pickles.' She let the smile come the rest of the way. 'I can recommend the roast beef, however, and there is plenty of lettuce and carrots.'

They stared at her blankly until Huggy, recovering first, managed to give a weak cheer.

'I have to go out tonight to a meeting,' Mrs. Summer continued briskly, 'but Mrs. Addams will be here, of course.' She looked at her watch. 'I must fly or I'll be late.'

They began to stack the dishes glumly. 'All that acting gone to waste,' Huggy moaned. 'And I didn't eat half enough, I was so busy yawning all the time.'

'Yeah,' John agreed. 'Heck, Mom always goes to bed with the birds, so we don't have to worry about her. Lucky for us Mrs. S. thought we were only planning a midnight feast!'

Candy suddenly set the dishes she had been stacking down on the table with a little thump. Ellen looked at her sharply. 'What's wrong? You look funny.'

'I—I—' Candy gulped. All the excitement of the day seemed to be inside her stomach boiling around.

'You're not going to be sick!' Huggy cried in dismay.

'N-no. I'm all right.' Candy took a determined grip on the dishes and walked steadily towards the kitchen. She must not be sick, she must *not*, or it would spoil everything. Mrs. Addams would put her straight to bed and fuss over her, popping in and out to be sure she was all right. Ordinarily, there was nothing Candy liked better than to be fussed over when she wasn't feeling well, but tonight was different. They had to go to Howard Hall to get Heather. But her stomach continued to churn like one of those big cement mixers—round and round.

'All right,' John announced in the kitchen, after an anxious glance at Candy's white face, 'all womenfolk out of the way. Us men are taking over tonight. Scram, you women. You too, Mom. We won't hide any dirty pans in the oven, and we'll scrub out the sink afterwards. Beat it, now.' He flapped a dish towel at them.

Candy sank miserably into a chair in the drawing-room while Ellen hovered about her suggesting remedies like warm milk or hot tea or baking soda, to all of which Candy shook her head with a shudder. John and Huggy came in when they had finished the dishes.

'Milka Magnesia, that's the thing,' said Huggy, his round face creased with worry. He shoved his glasses up on his nose and peered intently at Candy. 'You don't look so hot, pal. Better let ole Doc Pindar get the Milka—'

'I'd better tell Mom,' John said worriedly. 'She'll fix you up.'

Candy shook her head stubbornly. 'I'll be all right in a minute.'

But at nine o'clock, when Mrs. Addams came in to announce bedtime, the cement mixer was going round faster than ever. When Candy got to the top of the stairs, she suddenly made a beeline for the bathroom and was sick.

Later, tucked up in her bed, she sadly watched Ellen change into jeans and a dark sweater. It was almost time to start for Howard Hall.

'I'm awfully sorry,' Ellen said. 'Wouldn't you rather I stayed with you while the boys go after Heather?'

'No.' Candy shook her head too hard and felt dizzy again. 'But promise you'll wake me up if I'm asleep when you get back.'

'I promise,' Ellen said solemnly. 'Why don't you try to drink some of that milk now?'

Candy shuddered.

Ellen patted the covers over her shoulders and then tip-toed across the room and cautiously opened the door. ''Bye,' she whispered, and slipped out into the hall, leaving Candy alone with her bedside lamp, the glass of milk and cookies, and a trembly feeling inside. She strained her ears for sounds of departure in the still night air—what if Mrs. Addams heard them from her bedroom and made them come back? But there were only the usual night noises, the squeaks and groans of an old house settling in for the hours of darkness.

And then something began to tug at one corner of her mind, like a puppy pulling at a bedspread. Something she had wanted to think about, but hadn't had time in the midst of all that had happened since they discovered the tunnel.

Something—something that she had read or heard? About
—what was it about? Painting! That was it! Candy could
feel her brain wrinkling in an effort to remember . . .

Suddenly she sat bolt upright, her eyes wide. Then she
had to lie down again because she felt so light-headed. But
the idea which had come to her wouldn't let her alone.
Pulling herself up cautiously, she sat on the edge of the
bed until her head felt better. The others would have gone
if she didn't hurry. Seeing the glass of milk, she seized it
and drank it down to stop the cement mixer motion inside.
A moment later she was tiptoeing down the steps to the
drawing-room, a little wobbly, but warm with excitement.

But the drawing-room was dark and empty and silent.
The others had already gone! It took a few moments to find
the right magazine because her fingers trembled so much,
but at last she pulled it out of the stack and leafed through it
until she had found what she wanted. Kneeling under the
light of the floor lamp, she skimmed quickly through the
story:

> Art-hungry citizens of New Bushey, a small town in
> northern Ohio, last week petitioned millionaire Peter Slavo
> to let townspeople occasionally view his private art collec-
> tion. But Mr. Slavo, for twenty years a recluse at his
> 'Brookfield' estate, turned them down flat. 'My paintings,'
> said Mr. Slavo in an open letter to the citizens of New
> Bushey, 'are more personal to me than my mail. I am sure
> nobody would have the effrontery to suggest that I expose
> the contents of my desk to a curiosity-seeking public.'
>
> New Bushey-ites were more amused than chagrined at Mr.
> Slavo's reply. 'Mr. Slavo,' was one citizen's reply, 'appears
> to believe that, like his mail, the paintings he has bought
> were meant expressly for his eyes alone. We find it hard to
> believe that artists like Roualt, Matisse and Picasso had Mr.

Slavo solely in mind when they painted the pictures Mr.
Slavo later bought. However, they *are* Mr. Slavo's pictures
now and if he does not care to share them with his neighbors, his neighbors can and will gladly make the trip to
Capitol City where the Modern Art Institute welcomes
visitors.'

Mr. Slavo is reputed to have a collection of at least fifty
modern paintings, possibly many more. A shrewd collector,
Mr. Slavo is said to have bought many of his pictures before
the artists' names became well known. In 1947 he was the
victim of accusations that some of his paintings were ac-
quired illegally, but the case was never brought to court. It
is believed that nobody but Mr. Slavo has set eyes upon any
of the paintings since they were carried into Brookfield and
hung in the private gallery.

Mr. Slavo . . . paintings . . . Modern Art Institute . . .
patrons . . . Uncle Guy . . . copycat . . . Heather locked in
. . . Friday night . . .

With a bound, Candy was on her feet and flying silently
up the carpeted stairs to her room. Jeans, sweater, sneakers
(no time for socks), flashlight—she must have a flashlight.
There ought to be one in the kitchen. Stuffing the cookies
from the plate into her pockets and pausing only to be sure
she had her Worry-Wort, she flew downstairs again,
rummaged in kitchen drawers without success, though she
borrowed a box of matches from one of them. She looked
around helplessly, and spied a big flashlight on top of the
refrigerator. Snatching it, she paused to consider how the
others proposed to get back into the house, but no matter—
they must have a key.

In a few moments, Candy had plunged into the woods.
The path to the log cabin was so well defined by now that
there was no danger of straying off it. If she ran, she would

surely catch up with the others before they went through the tunnel.

But when she got to the log cabin, there was no sign of them. She surely couldn't be far behind. She must hurry along through the tunnel and find them on the other side to tell them what she had discovered. Why, they might be able to do something about . . .

She slipped into the tunnel and ran, bent over, through the passage. It was scary, being in here alone at night, but the thought of the others just ahead of her made her feel brave. Besides, she had her Worry-Wort in her pocket under the cookies, and he was a good-luck piece, wasn't he? She emerged cautiously from the tunnel under the piled-up logs and called softly. There was no answer. They had already started through the Howard woods!

With an inward quake, she went into the trees. But perhaps any minute Addle would sense her presence and come running back to greet her. She longed to feel his cold wet muzzle in her hand and the comfort of his silky body trotting along beside her. She wouldn't be a bit frightened anywhere in the world if Addle was with her. Winking her flashlight on and off to be sure she was still on the dimly-marked path, she went ahead slowly, nibbling on one of the cookies. She must be getting close to Howard Hall by now.

A root tripped her and sent her sprawling. The flashlight was jolted out of her hand. Getting to her knees, she groped for it, fighting down a feeling of panic when she didn't immediately find it. Wait a minute—the box of matches! She fumbled in her pocket amongst the cookies, got them out, and struck one. The trees were eerie in the dim flare and the night pressed in on her. There it was!—it had flipped right over another root. Thankfully, she picked it up and scrambled to her feet.

She really would have to hurry now to catch up to the others. Keeping the flashlight on, she hastened forward between the trees. It was spooky, all right, but even if she didn't catch up with John and Ellen and Huggy on the path, she would find them in the little patch where they had waited for Heather that afternoon.

Candy came to a tremendous log and started to climb over it when she stopped short. Surely there had been no log on the path earlier today.

Then . . . She stood perfectly still on top of the log.

Then . . . she was lost in Howard Woods . . .

15

INSIDE HOWARD HALL

NONSENSE, SHE scoffed. She *couldn't* be lost. She'd been right on the path when she dropped the flashlight— When she dropped the flashlight . . . She tried to remember. Had she fallen a little sideways and then when she found the flashlight, gone off the wrong way? And if so, which way had she gone from the path? For a moment, her brain wouldn't work at all. It felt like pie dough in her head. She stared around at the awful trees, the menacing trees that bent over her.

'Stop it!' she told herself sternly. 'Stop it right this instant!

They're just trees, ordinary trees, with baby squirrels and chipmunks asleep in them. And Heather came through here in the middle of a thunderstorm. That was *much* worse, but *she* wasn't afraid. Now think what to do! I must have gone left from the path because the flashlight was a little to the left of where I fell. Does that make sense? I don't know, but anyway, I *think* I went left. So now I'll go right for a while and see if I can't run across the path.'

She decided to eat another cookie to keep her teeth from chattering, and gave the Worry-Wort a good rub on his nose for luck—Huggy said it worked best when you rubbed its nose. Then, the big torch shining ahead, she started off to the right. Of course, ordinarily, in books you were always supposed to stay in one spot when you got lost and let somebody find you. But not when that somebody might be Uncle Guy! She hurried on. And on.

At last she stopped, bewildered. She surely must have crossed the path by this time if she was going in the right direction. What should she do now? The night-stirrings and scutterings in the branches were too terrifying for her to stay still very long. Candy cut back to the left, but on a diagonal that should bring her close to Howard Hall. Once she heard the toot of an automobile horn that seemed to come from somewhere in front of her. That must be at Howard Hall, unless she was way off and was approaching the road. She snapped off the flashlight and felt her way along.

By this time she was thoroughly-way-down-to-her-toes frightened. She could hear her heart hammering away so loudly that it sounded like a whole row of drums in a marching band. She ate the last three cookies one after the other, and then hurried on, one hand clutching tightly at the polished smoothness of the little Worry-Wort. The woods seemed just a bit brighter now, as though there might be a moon above the thick foliage.

She went on for what seemed like hours, but when she flicked on the flashlight to see what time it was, her watch showed only 10.45.

'WHO'S THERE?' A powerful flashlight beam sprang up, catching her and holding her in its cruel light.

Candy froze, her own flashlight dropping from her hand. Uncle Guy!

'Who is it?' Uncle Guy demanded. 'Come out of those trees. Who are you?'

There was nothing to do but move forward. After a dozen steps, she found that she had been standing only a few feet from the front lawn of Howard Hall.

'I-I'm lost,' she said, and to her own surprise she burst into a flood of tears.

Uncle Guy stood looking fixedly at her while she sobbed. 'How did you get in here?'

Candy sobbed harder to give herself time to think.

'All right,' said Uncle Guy. 'You're not lost any longer, but you are certainly trespassing. How did you get in here and where are you from?'

'I—I lost my dog,' Candy wailed. 'And—and I came to look for him, but I can't find him.'

'You came at *night* to look for a dog? Come on, tell me the truth.'

'No, I came after dinner, but I got l-lost in the woods and I c-can't find my little d-dog.' She could feel his eyes hard on her.

'Who came with you?' he demanded harshly.

'N-nobody. The—the other kids were mad at me and said they didn't like my old dog anyway 'cause he had f-fleas.' She broke into fresh sobs.

'And what made you think your dog would be here? You're from Summer House, I suppose?'

'Well, I looked everywhere over there and c-couldn't find him, so I—I thought may be he'd wandered out our front gate and into yours b-by mistake.'

'Our gate is always kept locked, though I suppose a small dog could squeeze through. And how did *you* get into the grounds?'

Candy had been expecting this and was all ready to say she had come through the gate, but if the gate was kept locked . . . ?

She found some more tears. 'Oh please, I'm sorry. I didn't *mean* to stay. I was going to look for my dog and go right back, only I got lost—'

'HOW DID YOU GET INTO THE GROUNDS?' It was a frightening voice, like the clang of metal.

'Why—why—up the tree, of course.'

'What tree?'

'The tree by the wall.' Candy talked fast. 'I climbed up the tree and got on the wall and then I just walked along till I found another tree on this side and shinnied down it.'

'And just where is this convenient tree?'

'I d-don't know now. If—if I did, I wouldn't be lost any more.' She ended on a wail.

A light flashed on the front porch of Howard Hall and a man stepped out. He wasn't as big as Uncle Guy, and there was something familiar about his figure, as though Candy had seen him somewhere before.

'What is it, Guy?' he asked. 'What is happening?'

'A lost kid from Summer House,' Uncle Guy said shortly. 'Says she lost her dog, too.'

'Oh.' Uncle Martin—Candy had recognized his voice—

came across the drive and the grass towards them. 'Then that *was* a dog barking a short while ago. Lucky you came out to investigate.'

'Was it *my* dog?' asked Candy, remembering to sniffle a bit. If Uncle Martin had heard a dog bark, it just had to be Addle, and that meant the others were around.

'Possibly,' said Uncle Guy. He seemed to be turning something over in his mind. 'I didn't find him.'

'Hadn't we better take the child home?' Uncle Martin asked.

'Yes—no.' Uncle Guy examined his watch in the beam of his torch. '*He's* coming at eleven.' He shook his head with annoyance. 'Look here, little girl, you're all right here, and I'll take you home in a little while, but I have a business appointment in a few minutes that I *must* keep. Come into the house—my wife will give you some hot milk or something.'

'But—what about my *dog*?'

'*Blast* your dog!' Uncle Guy almost yelled it, and then he recovered himself and went on in softer tones. 'We'll find your dog tomorrow. For heaven's sake, Martin, take this little cry-baby in to Ruth. I can't stand her another minute. Do get her out of the way.'

Little cry-baby! Candy thought indignantly. She ought to stamp on his foot for that.

'Come on, child,' Uncle Martin said gently, taking her by the hand. 'You must be worn out. I remember being lost in the woods one time, but that was in the daylight and I wasn't half as brave as you.'

'Hurry up, Martin!' snapped Uncle Guy. 'I hear his car.'

Candy tried to trail behind to get a look at the car. Always get the other fellow's licence number, her father kept telling

L

her mother. Of course, he meant when there was an accident, but if you got a licence number, you could find out who owned the car—that's what her daddy said. She thought she knew who owned *this* car, all right, but she ought to have some proof.

'Go *on*!' Uncle Guy gave her an ungentle push that propelled her up the porch steps. Candy bit her lips to keep from screaming at him. Just wait, she promised herself, just *you* wait, Uncle Guy, you—you thief!

The front door opened upon a little vestibule, beyond which was a great wide hall with a curving staircase going up on the left side. The hall itself looked shabby and dim and cold, though Candy thought it was probably the kind of thing her mother would exclaim over. There were some big marble busts of Romans or something—the kind with boiled-egg eyeballs, and even a suit of armour that Candy would have liked to investigate, but Uncle Martin kept her moving towards the back of the house. All the doors along the hall were closed.

'What a *big* house!' Candy said, trying to hold back. She could hear a car stopping outside the house.

'It was once a gracious one, for all its ridiculous exterior,' said Uncle Martin sadly. 'My wife used to say . . .'

His wife! Heather hadn't said anything about her. Maybe she was dead. Candy stopped and stared at Uncle Martin. He looked like the kind of uncle who would always bring a present when he came to visit. His eyes were a sad brown, but his eyebrows made funny peaked roofs over them. Again the feeling that she had seen him somewhere before swept over Candy.

'Please come along, child. My brother—' They reached the end of the hall and Uncle Martin swung open a door on the right, but not before Candy's quick eyes had seen

another door straight ahead—the back door, of course! The
one they had watched Aunt Ruth unlock that afternoon.
But Candy's heart sank. The huge bolt on the door was
driven securely home. No matter how many keys John had,
none of them would be of any use as long as the bolt was
closed.

Uncle Martin snapped on a light to reveal a big old-
fashioned kitchen with a fireplace on one side. A gleaming
white stove and refrigerator looked oddly lost and out of
place in the high-ceilinged room.

'If you will wait here, I'll get my brother's wife,' Uncle
Martin said. He hesitated, examining Candy's face intently.
'I wonder . . .' He seemed to make up his mind and began
speaking fast in a low voice. 'Could you give a message to
Mrs. Summer when my brother takes you home tonight?
The only thing is—my brother *must not know*.' His sad brown
eyes pleaded with her to understand.

Candy nodded eagerly. 'Don't worry. I wouldn't tell *him*
anything. And we're going to tell Mrs. S. about Heather,
anyway . . .'

Uncle Martin looked at her in astonishment. 'How did
you—? Never mind now. Yes, tell her about Heather and
say that I need her. Now. Tonight. It's very important.
But she shouldn't come alone—' He stopped short, listening
to a sound in the hall. 'I'll have to go. Don't be frightened
of my brother's wife. She's cross-tempered, but she would
never harm anyone.' He patted Candy gently on the head,
and went quickly out.

Candy waited for a moment and then tiptoed quietly to
the door. There were muffled sounds from the front of the
house. Candy pushed the door open a few inches and peered
out. Down the length of the hall and dwarfed by its size were
Uncle Guy and a scrawny taller man with his raincoat collar

pulled up and his wide-brimmed hat pulled down. His clothes looked as though he had stuffed them into a Salvation Army bag and then changed his mind and pulled them out again. His narrow shoulders were stooped, and he had a knobby awkward appearance. Uncle Martin was hastening towards him and Uncle Guy, and then they all went up the curving staircase, the murmur of their voices echoing in the barren hall.

Quick as a flash, Candy was at the back door, tugging at the bolt. It wouldn't budge. She gripped the knob with both hands and pulled with all her strength. The stiff bolt gave just a little. Above her she heard the tap-tap of high heels beginning to descend the stairs. With an inward cry of rage, she gave one more ineffectual tug at the bolt, but then she had to slip back into the kitchen, where she huddled in a high-backed rocking-chair near the fireplace and stared at the dead ashes, waiting for Aunt Ruth. She'd have to get rid of her, somehow, and then get that door unbolted or—find Heather. She almost jumped at this idea. Heather was at the top of that turret thing, and the turret thing was at this very end of the house. Maybe she could get to it from the kitchen—if she could get rid of Aunt Ruth. There were two doors in the opposite wall . . . If only she had paid more attention to those diagrams in the diary!

The tapping high heels sounded loud now, and the door from the hall swung open. Aunt Ruth, in a tight black dress and exuding a spicy perfume, came in, looking very cross indeed. She slammed the door behind her.

'Hel-hello,' Candy said, trying to look pitiful and meek. She managed a sound that would do for a sob.

'What's your name?' Aunt Ruth scowled at her.

'Candy Bascombe. I got l-lost.'

'Well, don't snivel. You're not lost any more.' She went

to the refrigerator, took out a carton of milk, poured some into a pan, and put it on the stove with a bang that splashed some of the milk over the sides. Candy changed her mind about Aunt Ruth's being like her Aunt Janet, even if they were both arty.

'I gather that you're from Summer House.'

'That's r-right.'

'Well, Mrs. Summer isn't going to be too happy with you for coming over the wall. I should have thought the first thing she told her boarders was to stay away from her wicked brothers.'

Candy let her eyes fly wide. 'Her brothers!'

Aunt Ruth studied her intently for a moment, but the sizzle of boiling milk suddenly claimed her attention. She snatched the pan off the stove, poured milk into a big tumbler and handed it to Candy.

'Now, look here, I don't believe for a moment you're the wide-eyed little innocent you pretend you are. I think you're a nasty little snoop. No child like you is going to climb a twelve-foot wall, with or without convenient trees, to look for a dog when there's no reason to think he's over here. You may have taken in Martin—he's dotty on children and an old fool to boot—and you may have fooled my husband for a minute, but you don't fool *me* for one second. Now what are you doing here? Who else is with you? Answer me!'

Candy's tongue stuck to the roof of her mouth. She took a quick swallow of milk. It was so hot that it burned her mouth and brought tears to her eyes. But Aunt Ruth was waiting inexorably for an explanation. There was no time to think.

'They—they told me he was here—the kids. They said they put him through your gate and the—the man who lived here would shoot him and have me arrested for not tying him up and—and—they hate me 'cause they say I'm stuck-up and a scaredy-cat and I'd be afraid to come after Addle, so I—I—well, I just *had* to come after that, but I didn't want to, and it got darker and darker and I couldn't find my way back—'

'Now wait a minute. Do you mean to say rules are so lax at Summer House that nobody has missed you? It doesn't sound like Lib to *me*. No matter what she thinks of her brothers, she would have called up long ago to inquire.'

Candy hadn't thought of that. She could feel her brain whirling around like a pinwheel.

'She went to a meeting tonight. And Mrs. Addams— that's John's mother—she'd believe any lies John told her. Of course, she's just the cook and you know what servants are like.' Candy crossed her fingers in her lap so that the lies wouldn't count. 'And anyway, they thought I'd gone upstairs to my room. I did that a couple of times already, and they never came near to see if I was all right.' Candy gulped down some of her milk.

'I don't wonder,' Aunt Ruth said acidly. 'My sympathies are with the other children.' She tapped her foot impatiently. 'Listen, Candy, I've got to go upstairs for a few minutes. You stay right here—drink your milk and then curl up and go to sleep if you can.'

Candy tried to look a little frightened and more than a little cowed. 'All right,' she said in a small lost voice. 'I'm so-o-o tired,' and she yawned.

Aunt Ruth stood frowning puzzledly at her for a moment, as though she wasn't entirely convinced. At last, however, she went clicketing out of the room and shut the door. Candy waited until the sound of heels had died completely away before she stirred. Then, moving carefully, she tiptoed to the door and listened. There was no sound in the hall. She grasped the knob and turned it gently. For a moment, she thought the door was stuck, and then her mouth fell open in consternation as she realized what had happened.

Aunt Ruth had locked the door!

16

SHENANIGANS

C ANDY TURNED slowly away from the door with tears of frustration in her eyes. If she just hadn't been so weak and trembly, she could have got that bolt open when she had the chance. But now— She suddenly remembered Heather, somewhere upstairs. Maybe if she found her, Heather would have an idea about letting the others in.

Darting across the big kitchen to the two doors, Candy yanked at the first one. It opened into a big pantry ranged with shelves full of dishes and cans of food. Backing out, she tried the other door. It stuck, but she jerked roughly at it until it gave with a grinding squeak.

Cool damp air, flavoured with the sharp smell of potatoes and apples and cheese, rushed at her. She blinked to accustom her eyes to the gloom. Then her heart sank, for it seemed to be only a storeroom. There were sacks on the floor and bins around the walls, and a big table cluttered with pans and jars. At regular intervals, narrow windows emitted feeble moonlight through their grime. Something about the position of the windows was peculiar—they seemed to be in a circle . . .

The turret! Of course! The storeroom was really the ground room of the turret. And Heather was somewhere at the top. There must be a way up. Candy stepped farther into the storeroom, pulling the door screechingly shut behind her. There were steps on the left side, she could see now, but what strange, terrifying steps! They spiralled like a barber's pole, up and up, disappearing into a round well in the ceiling. The diagrams from the diary flashed across her mind—the cross-eyed squiggles in the turrets were the circular stairs! As Candy approached, she saw that they also went down to blackness through a well in the floor.

Suppressing a shudder, Candy gingerly stepped on the little platform that partially covered the hole in the floor, and began to mount. The steps were of metal, like fire escapes, and there was an iron rail to hold tight to. Candy's sneakers made little sound on the steps, and she went as quickly as she could, around and up, around and up. Above the ceiling of the storeroom the steps, still spiralling upwards, were now enclosed in a narrow tube. She came to a little platform and leaned against the cold stone of the outer wall, feeling dizzy from going round and round. There was a small window in the wall, but it was so grimy that she couldn't see anything through it except the vague outline of trees against the lighter sky. Were the kids still out there, she wondered, or had they tried to get in the back door and then gone home when they failed? No, she decided, they wouldn't give up that easily. And if they heard her talking to Uncle Guy out on the lawn, they would never go off leaving her here. Somehow, they would get her and Heather out of this house.

With a lighter heart, Candy began to mount the next step, when she saw that there was a door opening off the platform. She turned the knob and peered in. A ghostly bed swathed in dust sheets loomed up. She shut the door quickly and moved on up the steps. She felt more secure climbing up in this tube-thing. And she must be almost to Heather's room, because this was the third floor she was coming to now.

At last she reached another platform and another door. There was a crack of light visible under the door and a glimmer at the keyhole.

'Heather?' she called softly.

There was no answer, but she heard a rustle inside. Candy tried the door. It was locked.

'Heather! It's me, Candy.' For an instant her heart dropped. What if it was someone else in the room?

Then the whisper came. 'Hel*lo*? I'm talking through the keyhole. Aren't you clever to find me! Is there a key out there?'

Candy shook her head, forgetting that Heather couldn't see her. 'No,' she whispered back through the keyhole.

'Oh dear, how beastly! Are all of you out there?'

'No, just me. They can't get in because the back door is bolted. Aunt Ruth locked me in the kitchen, only I—'

'But how did *you* get in the house?'

'Uncle Guy caught me.' Candy felt uneasy—they should be *doing* something instead of talking.

Heather laughed softly. 'Was that you? I heard it from my window. I say, what a jolly good actress you are! Isn't this a lark?'

'No,' said Candy, remembering the awful time in the woods. 'I mean, yes, now it is. Listen, I've got an idea. There's another room down below this one. Maybe it has a key that will fit.'

'You clever girl! Run quickly and see.'

Run quickly! She'd be lucky not to break her neck and tumble all the way down to the cellar, round and round and round. But she felt cheered now that she had found Heather, and hurried as fast as she could down to the ghostly bedroom and opened the door. Fumbling at the inside of the lock, she felt a rod of metal, but in her eagerness to pull it out, she dropped it. It bounced with a little tingling noise. She dropped on her knees and felt around for it. The floor was spider-webby, but she didn't let herself think about it. Then her fingers closed around the bit of metal, and she got to her feet, holding the key tightly in her sweaty fingers.

Hurry, hurry, she said with each step upwards. Hurry, hurry. But when she got to Heather's door, she changed it to Careful, careful. If she dropped the key now it wouldn't stop until it got to the cellar, and going down to the cellar was something she would *not* do.

The key went into the lock, all right, but it wouldn't turn. Candy had been so sure her idea would work that she couldn't believe it. She wiggled the key this way and that way, but the lock remained fast.

'Slip it under the door,' Heather whispered. 'I'll try from this side.'

Candy removed the key with great care and knelt on the

platform, trying not to look down the stairwell. The crack under the door was not very large, but near the jamb was a wider place. Candy inserted the key and pushed. About halfway through, it stuck fast.

'Bother,' Heather muttered. 'Half a minute. I'll get a knitting needle.'

Candy wondered what in the world a knitting needle could be, but then Heather's footsteps came back, and a moment later Candy saw the steel point of a knitting pin probing under the door. The key moved a trifle. Candy put out a hand to give it another push, narrowly missing being stabbed by the knitting needle-pin.

Desperately they worked until Candy felt clammy, and at last the key squeaked through. She could hear Heather trying it in her side of the door, the scritch-scratch loud in the darkness.

'Oh blazes,' Heather said, withdrawing the key. 'Something has gummed inside, I think. I say, I wonder if it would work on the other door!'

Her quick footsteps retreated across the floor of her room. The other door? Candy puzzled. Then there must be a door to the rest of the house. Of course! She had wondered how Aunt Ruth climbed those dreadful fire-escapey stairs in her high heels—not Aunt Ruth! Probably nobody had come up those steps for years and years. Maybe she was the first one for twenty years!

'I say, Candy,' came Heather's whisper, 'the key opens the other door. I'll nip out that way and meet you below. Wait, though, I'll just toss another note out of the window to your gang. Golly, won't Uncle Guy be *cross* when he finds out! Am I really going to stay at your house all night?'

'Yes, yes, only hurry! And be careful!'

'Righto.'

Candy wiped her clammy forehead and started down the winding stairs once more. She wished Heather would take this adventure a little more seriously. Of course, she didn't know all the things about Uncle Guy that were in the diary. All she thought was that Uncle Guy was going to be cross with her. Cross! Candy shivered in the gloom . . .

The warning screech of the door below her froze Candy in her tracks. She had just reached the platform in front of the door to the ghostly room. Peering down through the iron staircase, Candy saw the light streaming from the kitchen into the storeroom, and a figure silhouetted in the doorway. Aunt Ruth!

'All right, come out of there.' Aunt Ruth's voice grated harshly. 'I knew you for a snoop the moment I set eyes on you. Come on out. Don't think I can't see you!'

Candy shrank back against the door. She couldn't see, she couldn't. It was a cheap grown-up trick to scare children out of their hiding places. Aunt Ruth couldn't see her way up here, in the dark, and as long as she didn't make any noise . . .

'Very well,' Aunt Ruth said, her voice shaking with rage. 'Either you come out of there this minute, or I'll lock this door and you can stay in the dark.'

Candy cringed against the door, felt it swing silently open behind her. Tremblingly, she stepped across the threshold of the ghostly room, remembering the spider-webby feel of the floor when she had scrabbled for the key. But spiders couldn't hurt you. Huggy wouldn't be afraid of spiders. He would probably whisper in their ears and tell them a better way to spin their webs! Cheered, she groped her way across the room, past the sheet-swathed bed. There must be another door to this room, like Heather's above.

'Or would you like me to get my husband?' Aunt Ruth's voice pursued her.

The dim light from the curtained windows grew a little brighter, as though the moon had sailed out from behind a cloud. It showed a door set in the wall!

'That settles it.' Aunt Ruth's loud furious voice was muffled by the floorboards. 'I shall lock this door and get my husband to attend to you.'

Candy reached the door and grasped the knob. Her fumbling fingers touched a key, but she didn't need it. The door gave! But just in case she might need it, she extracted the key from the lock.

Below, she heard the protesting squeak of the storeroom door closing, but she didn't care. In another moment she would be out of the turret, and then . . . She didn't know what then, but at least—Puzzled, she stood still and listened. There were queer, muffled poundings coming from below, and shouting. What was happening? Aunt Ruth must have discovered Heather! But what—

In consternation, Candy pushed open the door and peered out. She had expected to come out into a sort of hall on the second floor, but instead she was in a small sitting-room, the chairs and long couch shrouded in dust sheets, like the bed in the room behind her. There was another door, though, and Candy crossed confidently towards it, key ready. A moment later she thanked her lucky stars for that piece of metal, for the door was locked. The key went in and turned easily. Below her, the banging and pounding still went on. What on earth was happening? Aunt Ruth couldn't be *beating* Heather, could she?

Frightened, Candy flung open the door and saw—Huggy and Ellen and Addle! They were just disappearing into a room up the hall on the opposite side. Almost at the same instant there came pounding footsteps from the floor above. Candy hastily closed her door except for a crack through which she could see the long wide dimly-lit hall with its staircase at her end.

Feet thundered down the stairs from above, and Uncle Guy came into view, his narrow face drawn into severe lines of anger. He flashed past her, going on down to the first floor. Instantly, a door across from her opened, and John shot out, followed by Heather. They clipped up the stairs, two at a time. Candy took out after them, but when she reached the top of the steps, they had already disappeared. She found herself looking straight ahead to a brilliantly lighted room at the far end of the hall. For a confused moment, she stood gazing at a conglomeration of easels, stacked canvases, large cupboards, expanse of curtained window—and the backs of two men! She darted into the nearest room . . .

There was a startled gasp in the darkness, then—

'Candy!' John breathed. 'Thank goodness! We were just coming after you. Are you all right?'

'Of course,' said Candy, panting.

A shrill sharp scream cut through the air.

'That's Ellen,' John said with satisfaction. 'What terrific lungs!'

'Listen,' warned Heather. 'There goes Uncle Martin down the stairs. Now let's—'

Candy put out a restraining hand. 'There's still another one. Mr. Slavo.'

'Who's—never mind, we've got to get him out of there.' Dimly, from below, they could hear doors opening and shutting. The pounding had stopped, but there were hurried footsteps up and down stairs, punctuated with Uncle Guy's harsh bellowing voice.

John opened the door a crack. 'Heather, you go on out and tell Mr. Slavo your uncle needs him,' he whispered. 'Hurry up. Then Candy and I'll go to the studio.'

'Righto,' Heather said, and slipped out.

Behind the closed door, Candy and John listened.

'Mr. Slavo!' Heather called shrilly. 'Mr. Slavo, come quickly! Uncle Guy wants you.'

There was another bloodcurdling scream from Ellen. Doors slammed. Uncle Guy cursed. Mr. Slavo's footsteps went heavily past the room and started down the stairs.

'Oh do hurry, Mr. Slavo!' Heather cried.

'Now,' said John. He opened the door and they slid out into the hall. They caught a glimpse of Mr. Slavo disappearing down the stairs, his hand firmly grasping Heather's shoulder.

'I don't understand all this,' John said, as they legged it towards the studio, 'but I intend to,' he added grimly.

Mr. Slavo had closed the door of the studio, but it was not locked. They burst in and stood panting a moment, leaning against the door. It was a large room with a skylight and the great curtained expanse of window they had seen from outside. Fluorescent tubes in the ceiling sprayed bright light everywhere. Mammoth cupboards filled one wall; the others were crowded with paintings. Still more canvases were stacked everywhere. A table was littered with tubes of colour and brushes and palettes. Another table held an untidy bundle of brown wrapping paper, a roll of canvas and paint rags.

But the thing that caught and held their eyes was a framed picture set on a large easel directly in front of them. It was quite unlike any of the other paintings around the room. Candy nodded briskly and began searching, searching with her eyes to find what she knew must be somewhere in the studio. But she didn't spot it.

'There should be another one just like it,' she said worriedly.

'My gosh, why?' John stared at the distorted figure in the painting. 'Isn't one enough? Look, her stomach's all out of kilter!'

Candy smiled because it was the same sort of thing she often said to her mother and father in the dozens of art galleries she had been dragged through. 'It's the feeling that's important,' she said.

'Umm. Well, my feeling is that something she ate threw her stomach out of joint. And great gravy, she's got two faces . . .'

'I know.' Candy began to prowl uneasily around the studio, fingering the canvases propped against the wall. 'Help me look for another one, John. We've got to hurry.'

John came to life. 'Sure, but will you tell me why?' He swung open the doors of the cupboards, shut them again, went over to inspect the roll of canvas on the table.

'Because one's a copy, that's why. Uncle Guy is selling the real one, the one that's supposed to go to the Institute, to Mr. Slavo! He's a thief!'

'Whew! How do you— Hey! What's this?' He pounced upon the bundle of brown paper wrappings lying on the table, and folded back the top layer. 'By jingo, look here,' he breathed, staring down at the partially-wrapped painting. 'It's *exactly* like the other one, even the frame!'

'That's the real one, then,' Candy declared. 'And Mr. Slavo is going to take it—' Candy looked suddenly at the door. They both heard running steps in the hall. John flopped the wrapping over the painting and jumped back. The door burst open.

'Quick!' cried Heather. 'Old Slavo's coming up the stairs, but I got away from him and came up the front turret. Come on with me!'

She turned and darted off to the left of the hall, Candy

M

right behind her. They dashed through an open door, and only then looked back for John. He was not in sight. The door of the studio was closed.

'Where did he go?' Candy gasped.

Heather shook her head, and put her fingers to her lips. Just before she swung the door silently shut, Candy caught a glimpse of Mr. Slavo's stooped form coming up the stairs at the far end of the hall.

They were in a large bedroom, but there were no ghostly sheets here. Heather took Candy's hand and led her through another door into a bathroom—a circular bathroom! They were in one of the turrets at the front of the house.

'Uncle Martin's room and bath,' Heather explained, and took her through another door.

Steps. Circular steps, winding down and down and down.

'But Mr. Slavo mustn't get away,' Candy said suddenly. 'And what about John?'

'I don't know,' said Heather. 'But something has happened to Uncle Martin.'

'Is he hurt?'

'No, but Uncle Guy is. He twisted Ellen's arm and slapped Huggy and knocked his specs off, and—and—' she suddenly giggled— 'and Uncle Martin bashed Uncle Guy right in the tummy! It was gorgeous! I left then because I saw Mr. Slavo was backing off towards the stairs. If it hadn't been for Auntie Ruth rushing out of the back turret room in her stocking feet and waving her shoes right in Mr. Slavo's face, I would have been able to warn you in time.'

Candy stopped dead on the stairs. 'But Mr. Slavo *must* not get away with the painting. We've got to stop him!' She turned and started back up the stairs.

They ran up the steps, through Uncle Martin's bathroom

and bedroom, and into the hall—straight into the arms of Uncle Guy.

At that moment they heard a car backfire in front of the house, the scrape of fast-turning wheels in gravel, and then the sound of the motor died quickly away. After all they had gone through, Candy realized with dismay that Mr. Slavo had made his escape with the Art Institute's latest $10,000 painting.

17

THE END OF IT ALL

'ALL RIGHT, you two, we're finished with hide-and-seek.'
Uncle Guy grasped Candy and Heather by an arm and
started marching them down the hall. 'And don't think you
can try any more tricks. I've got your mangy little dog
stowed away in a locked closet. First bit of trouble I have
with any of you . . . Do you understand?' He shook
Candy's arm almost out of her shoulder.

They went quietly enough down the steps to the second
floor. Aunt Ruth, her sleek hair half coming down, and with

a heel missing from one of her shoes, met them with a vicious look at Candy.

'Shut up, Ruth,' Uncle Guy snapped before she could say a word.

Uncle Martin was sitting on a bench holding Ellen's and Huggy's hands protectively. There was no sign of John. Candy's heart lifted.

'Are we all here?' Uncle Guy asked with a sneer. 'You two sit over there on the mourners' bench with the rest.' He gave Candy and Heather a shove. 'A pretty sight, I must say. Now suppose you tell me what you think you've all been doing tonight?'

Candy spoke up quickly. 'We came to rescue Heather because you locked her in, only I got lost and—'

'*Not* you.' Uncle Guy glared at her. 'I've had enough of your slippery tongue. You,' and he pointed at Huggy, disconsolate in his twisted glasses, one lens up to his eyebrow, the other resting on his cheek. 'What's your name?'

'That's John,' Candy cut in. She remembered talking about John to Aunt Ruth, and Aunt Ruth might start wondering where John was.

'Who, me?' Huggy asked groggily. 'I'm—'

'Tell him, *John*,' Candy repeated.

Uncle Guy strode over and slapped Candy on the ear. 'Not another word from you!' he roared.

It was the first time anybody had ever struck Candy. She kicked Uncle Guy as hard as she could on the shin.

'Why, you—' He started for her, his hands shaking.

Uncle Martin was suddenly between them, his hand lashing out in a stinging slap at Uncle Guy's face. Uncle Guy fell back a step in sheer astonishment, staring down at his smaller brother.

'I've never learned to use my hands for fighting,' Uncle

Martin said fiercely, 'but if you lay one finger on a child here, I shall start on you, big as you are. Furthermore, I'll tell everything. Do you understand? Everything!'

The children gave a ragged cheer.

Uncle Guy laughed nastily. 'You'll never touch *me* with your story.' But he recoiled another step, and his hand crept up to his cheek which showed red from Uncle Martin's hand. 'Nevertheless, the child forced her way into my house and—'

'I didn't either,' Candy retorted. 'You practically shoved me through the door.'

'You are forgetting,' Uncle Guy said with an effort at control, 'that I still have your little dog, and—' He broke off as Uncle Martin started towards him again. 'I'm within my rights. This is my house and you've broken into it late at night. You, John. Tell me what all this is about.'

Huggy gulped. 'Well, we—we talked to Heather—uh—over the wall one day, and she said you were awful strict, see, and—and . . .' He looked around desperately to Candy for help.

'Go on,' said Uncle Guy grimly. 'The little girl isn't talking any more today.'

But Candy didn't even hear him. She had heard a new sound in the house.

'What was *that*?' Aunt Ruth demanded sharply.

It was the sound of feet on the stairs. They all turned and watched to see who was coming up.

'Mrs. S.' the children shouted.

Uncle Martin looked as though he couldn't believe his eyes. 'Jacqueline!' He started forward with arms outstretched, only to come to a faltering stop.

Mrs. Summer and Mrs. Addams, followed by John, advanced on the group.

'Good evening, children. Good evening, Martin.' Mrs. Summer ignored Uncle Guy and Aunt Ruth, who were staring at her and Mrs. Addams, thunderstruck.

'He's got Addle locked up,' Ellen said. 'He's going to hurt Addle!'

'Oh no he's not,' said Mrs. Addams, walking towards Uncle Guy. 'Are you, dear Guy? You thought that you had frightened me away for good, didn't you? But I've come back, you see.' She changed to French and rattled off a spate of words unintelligible to the children. But Uncle Guy apparently understood. He handed a key to Mrs. Addams and motioned to a door at the far end of the hall. Mrs. Addams gave the key to John, who hurried to the door and unlocked it. Addle leaped out, almost knocking John down, and then rushed up and down the hall until he caught Uncle Guy's scent. His hair bristled, and he growled.

'Here, Addle,' John called. 'It's all right now. He won't hurt you.'

Addle backed off, making slow snarling sounds in his throat, his eyes fastened longingly on Uncle Guy.

'I've always disliked this gloomy hall,' Mrs. Summer said. 'Let's go up to your studio, Mart.'

Uncle Martin nodded. 'Yes, I think it is up to me to—Lib, will you take Heather to your house tonight and keep her there safe?'

'Of course. We're taking you, too. I should have realized long ago that you wanted to break away. He's run through all the money, hasn't he, Mart?'

'Aren't you forgetting it was his to run through?' asked Aunt Ruth jeeringly. 'Remember that old Mr. Howard left everything to Guy. And Martin hasn't had *too* hard a life while Guy worked to keep him fed and clothed. All Martin has done is to cover fifty acres of canvas with worthless daubs which he couldn't even sell at Woolworth's.'

'He could so!' Candy cried. 'And I'm going to save up and buy one, myself!'

'So am I,' Ellen chimed in.

'Me too,' said Huggy. 'I've got a buck-fifty already.'

'Not so worthless after all, you see,' Mrs. Summer said. 'But the past is finished now. Mart can paint all he wants at my house.' She put out her hand to her brother and drew him towards the steps. 'Perhaps you would even enjoy being a partner with Jacqueline and me in our new plans. We'll need an art teacher.'

Aunt Ruth gave a hoot of laughter. 'What a joke! Martin a painting master to a bunch of jam-fingered ten-year-olds.'

Uncle Martin smiled sadly. 'I should like nothing better, Lib, but—' He straightened his shoulders. 'I have decided what I must do. It's the only way. I suppose I could even be sent to prison, though I did the only thing possible . . .'

'Hush,' said Mrs. Summer. 'Wait till we get to the studio.'

'By all means.' Uncle Guy gave an ugly laugh. 'Let's just wait. But I might mention that I saw Mr. Slavo go out of here with his package a short while ago. You're going to have a hard time proving *I* had anything to do with the deal. After all, who does the painting in this house?'

They all went up the stairs, the children and Addle solemnly bringing up the rear.

'What an extraordin'ry night,' Heather whispered to Candy, her eyes dancing. 'Am I *really* going to come and live with you? And who *is* the lady who ticked off Uncle Guy? She's smashing! She *won't* let Uncle Martin go to prison, will she?'

'Of course not,' Candy said stoutly. 'And you're going to

live with us because Mrs. S. is your cousin, too. She's Uncle Martin's sister.'

'How simply *super*!'

When they reached the studio, Mrs. Summer flung the door open, and they all crowded through.

'Welcome to Martin's Art Gallery,' said Uncle Guy with a sneer. 'The home of all the Might-Have-Beens but Not-Quites.'

But nobody paid attention to him. Uncle Martin was standing stockstill staring fixedly at the framed picture on the easel, the painting of the woman with two faces and a double-jointed stomach. Mrs. Summer and Mrs. Addams and John were watching Uncle Martin's face, and Candy, Ellen and Heather looked at the four of them in bewilderment. Aunt Ruth was sitting on the edge of a table, swinging her foot in its heel-less slipper. Addle sniffed suspiciously at a tube of crimson madder which had fallen to the floor. He licked at it once or twice, backed off, came forward for another sniff.

'Ah,' said Uncle Guy. 'You are looking at the latest acquisition of the Modern Art Institute. Some ten thousand dollars were supplied by our excellent patrons to pay for that, but, do you know, there is not one of them who will ever fully appreciate what he has got for his money. *Isn't that right, Martin?*'

Uncle Martin gave no indication that he heard.

'These people with money love to pour it out on Culture, with a capital C, but they don't know enough about art to fill a rain barrel. They have to put their faith in Guy Howard, who, I might say, provides for them handsomely . . .'

Candy had opened her mouth to give a stinging retort on behalf of her mother and father, but she closed it again without saying a word. There was something going on here that she didn't understand, and in the last few days she had learned that sometimes it is better not to blurt out all that you know.

'. . . provides for them handsomely, I say. *Don't you agree, Martin?*'

There was silence except for Addle's tongue lapping at the crimson madder. Mrs. Summer put out her hand and touched Uncle Martin's sleeve. He turned to look at her, his eyes brightening with a smile.

'*Well, Martin?*' Uncle Guy said.

'I agree, Guy,' Uncle Martin replied, and his voice was strong and sure. 'You have provided for them handsomely. I see no reason to drag the family name in the mud. But Heather and I are going home with Lib, now, tonight.'

'Well, isn't that *touching*!' Aunt Ruth hopped down from the table. 'Now if you *kind* people will excuse us, we have a painting to deliver to the Institute tonight. I'm going on down to tidy up, Guy.' She delivered an acid smile to the rest. 'Just make yourselves at home, though, the way you've been doing all along. You might close the door on your way out.' She started to stalk across the room, forgetting about her heel-less slipper, and almost fell flat on her face. Addle growled deep in his throat. Candy felt like giggling and then suddenly she didn't any more. She almost felt sorry. Poor Aunt Ruth. Imagine having to *be* somebody like that.

Aunt Ruth glared at all of them and then continued her stalking-out process, but her steps sounded tip-tap, *klonk* . . . tip-tap, *klonk*. She slammed the door behind her.

Uncle Guy was folding sheet after sheet of brown paper around the painting which he had lifted down from the easel. 'One can't be too careful with a work of art.' He sealed the package with brown tape, and picked it up jauntily. 'Well, see you all at the Institute on Sunday for the Big Showing. Eh, afraid I can't invite you to call again here at the house. You see, I just completed the sale of the old place this afternoon.' He smiled mockingly at Mrs. Summer and Uncle Martin.

'I know,' said Mrs. Summer. 'Jacqueline and I bought it.'

'You!' Uncle Guy's face got very red.

'Yes. Our lawyer managed the affair for us. We're expanding into a school.'

Uncle Guy pulled himself together. 'Well, isn't that fine. Think of the fun you'll have moulding all of those grimy little characters—' he waved at the children '—into grimy little adults. I wish you well.' With a sweeping bow, he went out the door. Addle gave a contented sigh and went back to examining the tube of crimson madder. He didn't care for the taste, but he had just discovered that if he pressed on the tube with his paw, an interesting oozy substance came out the other end.

Mrs. Summer put her fingers to her lips before the children could burst out with questions. They sauntered about the room examining Uncle Martin's paintings until they heard the station wagon zoom into life and go off in a spit of gravel.

'Now, what gives?' demanded Huggy, trying to straighten his glasses. 'I've just about died, trying to keep my mouth shut all this time.'

'Where did you get to, John?' asked Candy. 'When Heather and I—'

'*Do* stop,' Heather begged. 'Somebody begin at the beginning. I don't know anything.'

'I'll start,' said Uncle Martin gravely. They all settled on chairs or cross-legged on the floor, and looked expectantly at him.

'It's very simple, really,' Uncle Martin said. 'Guy asked me to copy a painting which he had just bought for his patrons so that he could hang the copy in the Institute and sell the real one to Mr. Slavo—for $6,000. He couldn't get more than that from Slavo, though he tried hard enough. Of course, I refused, but Heather arrived from England just at that time. Guy threatened . . .' Uncle Martin looked hesitantly at Heather. . . . 'Guy has sometimes hurt people when he couldn't get his way. I thought it was better to agree to copy the painting than to run any risk of an accident to Heather. You see, there is no law against copying a painting as long as you don't try to palm it off on someone as the real thing. I was sure I could get Heather safely away long before I finished the copy. Then I would simply leave this house and Guy for ever. But Guy must have realized what I was planning. He and Ruth moved in immediately, and never left us alone together for a moment. They even had the telephone extensions taken out, leaving just one telephone and that one in their room where I couldn't get at it.'

'So I discovered,' John said. 'That's where I called up Mom and Mrs. S. tonight when the rest of you were mixing it up in the hall. Boy, I never went up and down so many circular stairs in my life! If it hadn't been for . . . uh . . . a map I happened to have, I'd have been lost, for sure.'

Then Candy related all of her part in the proceedings, with many stops and interruptions, especially from Huggy, who got so excited that he almost rubbed the lenses off his glasses. 'Well, little old Needle-nose,' he said admiringly when she had finished. 'What a gal!' John and Ellen and Heather all beamed approvingly on her, and Candy felt flushed with happiness.

Then Heather started in with her part. 'After I got out with Candy's key, I ran downstairs, but when I got to the back door, I heard Aunt Ruth screeching up the turret stairs at Candy, so I locked the kitchen door, and finally managed to slip the bolt on the back door, and there were John and Ellen and Huggy on the doorstep. We had to make plans to rescue Candy, but just then Aunt Ruth discovered that she was locked in and really began to shriek. So we cut upstairs, but we heard Uncle Guy coming, and had to dodge into the first rooms we came to. John and I were going to dig out the lock in my room to get to Candy, while Ellen and Huggy distracted anyone who needed distracting. But when we got to the second floor—'

'Third floor,' corrected Huggy.

'Second floor, the way we count in England. Ground floor, first floor, second floor.' She ticked them off on her fingers.

'All right, all right, you win,' said Huggy.

'. . . When we got up to the *top* floor, to my room, there came Candy bursting in right behind us, not needing rescuing at all, and giving us rather a start—'

'*Rather* a start!' John snorted. 'I almost fainted dead away.'

'Then I started to scream,' Ellen said. 'We thought we'd better fetch Uncle Martin down in case Uncle Guy got rough—we didn't know Mr. Slavo was up there too.'

'And then everything got all mixed up,' said Huggy, 'with Uncle Guy finding us, and Uncle Martin slugging Uncle Guy, and then Uncle Guy slugging Uncle Martin, and my gosh, will you look at my specs!'

'And Uncle Guy had to leave Aunt Ruth locked in the kitchen,' Ellen gurgled, 'because Heather had taken the key, and Aunt Ruth had to climb up those horrible circular stairs, and broke her heel and ruined her stockings—'

'But the awful thing is,' Candy cried, jumping to her feet, 'we let Mr. Slavo get away with that painting! And now

Uncle Guy has taken the copy off to the Institute after all, but there's something funny about that, I know . . .' She suddenly whirled on John, her mouth open. 'John Addams, what *were* you doing when Heather and I ran out—'

'Switching the paintings, of course.' John looked pleased with himself. 'And then hiding in that big cupboard while Mr. Slavo made off with the wrong painting. He paid Uncle Guy six thousand dollars for Uncle Martin's copy!'

'Yippee!' yelled Huggy, and then sobered. 'Gee-money, though, Uncle Guy's got the six thousand. That's a pitiful pity, I say.'

'He's welcome to it,' said Uncle Martin, 'if he can hang on to it. Mr. Slavo is a shrewd customer. I think we can count on him to get his own back, sooner or later. He also has quite a lot of influence, for a recluse. He'll see to it that the Institute will soon be looking for a new Curator.'

For the first time since Mrs. Addams came into the house, Uncle Martin looked squarely at her. All the others had started talking amongst themselves, but Candy was still puzzling over the strange familiarity of Uncle Martin's face.

'Jacqueline,' Uncle Martin said, and she smiled up at him. 'I know why you went away—to put John beyond Guy's reach. You were afraid he would run John's life too, the way he has always run mine—ever since we were children. But I've broken away from him at last. He'll never make trouble for any of us again.' Uncle Martin took Mrs. Addams's hand. 'Jacqueline, if you knew how I searched for you and John after you left! Do you think you could—'

Mrs. Addams smiled into his eyes and held out her other hand to him. 'Of course, Martin.' Then she drew the hand away and put it on John's shoulder to draw him over. 'John dear, would it be a great shock to learn that Addams is really your second name instead of your last? You were named for your grandfather, John Addams Howard.'

Candy stared from one to another in bewilderment. And then she understood why Uncle Martin looked so familiar to her. Except for his paler colour and his greying hair, it was John's face all over again, even to the funny eyebrows that went up in little wings right in the middle!

Mrs. Summer suddenly clapped her hands together. 'Who's for that midnight spread?'

'Hoo-ray!' shouted Huggy.

'Hoo-ray!' shouted all the others.

As they trooped out of the studio, Candy suddenly stopped. 'By the way, Mrs. Ad—Mrs. Howard, what was all that French you said to Uncle Guy when he gave you the key to let Addle out?'

John's mother smiled and her black eyes sparkled. 'If you study your French very well, you might know some day. Although,' and she winked, 'if I ever hear you using such language, any of you, I'll wash all your mouths out with soap!'

The midnight feast started promptly at midnight, with everybody sitting on the floor around the coffee table in the drawing-room. A fire crackled cheerfully in the grate, while arms reached out for roast beef, devilled eggs, celery, tomatoes, potato chips, pudding or fruit, and tongues chattered incessantly. John, sitting beside his newly-found father, looked a little dazed, but Heather acted as though she had exciting adventures every day of her life. Ellen passed plates of food around, and Huggy talked with his mouth full. Candy sat with her knees drawn up to her chin, looking happily at everybody and nibbling now and then from the plate beside her. Mrs. Summer and John's mother beamed generally on all of them. And Addle, admitted to the house as a special treat, was behaving admirably in hopes of being invited back again. He cast longing glances at a soft armchair, but remained quietly by Huggy's side, eating gratefully whatever came his way.

'Hey,' cried Huggy between bites of an enormous beef sandwich, 'we forgot to drink a toast! I say, here's to John and his Mom and Pop!' He raised his glass of milk in the air.

'And Mrs. S.—I mean my Aunt Lib!' said John, his sunburned face glowing. He held his glass up.

'And Heather. Here's to all the Howards present!' Ellen added her glass.

'And to the Howards' good friends, who saved the day!' said Uncle Martin, smiling happily and raising his coffee cup.

Addle whined softly.

'And specially Addle,' laughed Candy, 'because he started the whole thing with a grey woollen sock!'

They all solemnly stood up and drank all the toasts all at once.

THE END